A Literary Offense

Elizabeth Penney

AnniesFiction.com

Books in the Secrets of the Castleton Manor Library series

Library of Congress-in-Publication Data
A Literary Offense/ by Elizabeth Penney
p. cm.
ISBN: 978-1-64025-195-3
I. Title
                        2017963680

AnniesFiction.com
(800) 282-6643
Secrets of the Castleton Manor Library™
Series Creator: Shari Lohner
Series Editor: Lorie Jones
Cover Illustrator: Jesse Reisch

10 11 12 13 14 | Printed in China | 9 8 7 6 5

Early-morning sunlight streamed through the trees, casting dappled shade on the patio. Faith Newberry leaned back in her chair with a sigh, closing her eyes against the welcome warmth. Summers in New England never seemed long enough, and Faith planned to savor every last moment. As librarian at Castleton Manor on Cape Cod, she was busy year-round. The respite offered by the former gardener's cottage tucked at the edge of the Victorian garden was a perk she treasured.

An odd series of squeaks and chattering noises caught her ear. She opened her eyes to see her tuxedo cat, Watson, chasing a creature with a small head and a long, lithe body.

What is that? Faith reared back in her seat, lifting her feet as the duo charged toward her.

Fortunately, they veered off, and the animal darted between several large pots holding tomato and basil plants.

Watson pressed his face between the pots, trying to force a path for his larger body.

"Cut it out, Rumpy," Faith said, using her pet name for the cat. "He might bite you." She lifted the cat and moved him a distance away. "I think you're just jealous that he has a tail." Watson's own tail was bobbed as the result of an accident years before.

Hissing sounds from behind the pots reinforced her theory that the animal might well attack Watson.

Moving slowly so as not to startle the creature, Faith pushed aside heavy-laden tomato branches and peered down.

A tiny tan face gazed back, the brown stripe across its eyes resembling a bandit's mask.

"Who are you?" she asked. Guests at Castleton Manor often brought their pets, but she'd never seen anyone with a ferret.

"Excuse me. Excuse me."

Faith looked toward the strident voice. A middle-aged woman with a blonde bob was bearing down on her like a tugboat—short, stout, and determined.

"Can I help you?" Faith asked, thankful she'd gotten dressed. She rarely had unexpected visitors at the cottage, so she often sat outside in the jersey shorts and T-shirt she wore to bed.

The woman eyed her up and down, adjusting her wire-rimmed glasses on her nose. "I hope so. I had Fitz a minute ago."

Faith reeled. Was the woman saying she was having fits? She appeared healthy enough, standing steady, feet planted wide. "I'm sorry. What did you say?"

With a huff, the woman jammed her fists onto her ample hips. "I was walking my ferret, Fitz, when he disappeared. I wondered if he came this way."

Faith pointed to the tomatoes. "He's hiding behind that pot. My cat chased him back there."

The woman scowled.

Faith introduced herself. "Are you staying at the manor?"

"I certainly am." The woman drew herself up proudly. "I'm Avis Roth." When Faith didn't react, she added, "*The* Avis Roth. With Benson, Ritter, and Noyes. The literary agency?"

"Oh, right. I've heard of them." Faith extended a hand. "Nice to meet you." Avis's hand was clammy and limp, and Faith quickly withdrew her fingers. She cleared her throat. "Let's get Fitz out of there so you can be on your way." *And I can get back to breakfast.*

But when Faith moved the plant pot aside, Fitz shrank back into the shadows, then darted along the wall and through a gap in the foundation lattice.

Avis crouched down, calling for the pet, but he refused to come out. She glared at Watson, who sat nearby watching the proceedings with interest. "It's your cat's fault," she snapped. "Put him inside."

Faith hastened to obey and deposited an indignant Watson in the kitchen.

But Fitz remained reluctant to emerge, despite his owner's increasingly desperate efforts.

Faith was all too aware of time ticking away. She was due at the library soon, and although no one made her punch a time clock, she hated to be late. "Maybe if we leave him, he'll come out later," she said.

Avis's reaction was so extreme that one might have thought Faith had suggested setting a bear trap. "That's a terrible idea." Face reddening, the agent waved a hand at the gardens between the manor and the cottage. "There are too many places for him to get lost. We'll never see him again."

Faith cringed. "I'm sorry. I have no idea how to take care of a ferret. I've only had cats."

"That's obvious." Avis crossed her arms, fuming. "I'm not leaving until Fitz is safe."

Help. Faith sent up a silent plea for assistance.

As if in response, a young man came striding across the lawn. She recognized him as Eban Matthews, one of the manor's gardeners.

"Good morning," he said, his tanned face breaking into an attractive grin. With a toss of his head, he shook his straight dark hair into place. "Would it bother you if I trim your shrubs, Miss Newberry? They're getting a little tall." He pointed to the foundation plantings, which indeed were nudging the mullioned windows.

Fitz chose that moment to make his strange chattering sound.

Eban cocked his head, listening intently. "Is that a ferret I hear?"

"Yes it is," Faith said. "He's under the cottage, and we can't get him out."

"Her cat scared him." Avis wrung her hands. "I have no idea what I'm going to do."

The gardener went to the lattice and proceeded to chitter back to the creature. Within a minute, Fitz emerged, allowing Eban to pick him up. "Here you are, ma'am."

"I'm Avis Roth," the woman grumbled as she reached into her skirt pocket and pulled out a leash. "Set him down, and I'll clip this on him."

Eban's eyes were wide as he set Fitz gently onto the tiles. "Avis Roth, the literary agent?"

"That's right." Avis attached the leash and stood. "I'll be off now." She made a brusque gesture for Eban to move aside.

"Um, Ms. Roth," Eban said, "I submitted a book to you at your request. It's called *Exposure*, and it's based on a true story about a deadly winter hiking trip in the White Mountains—"

"Lots and lots of people send me books." Avis barged ahead, tugging at the leash. "If you haven't gotten a response, then it's a no." She turned and sent him the briefest of glacial glares. "I'd take a few writing classes, if I were you." Then it was face forward once more, and the pair trundled away.

Eban gave a huge exhale, his shoulders slumping. "That didn't go so well, did it?" Then he brightened. "But how many writers can say they rescued an agent's ferret? Maybe she'll give my book another read." He sagged again. "Who am I kidding? That will never happen. My book probably stinks."

Faith was glad she wasn't a writer, only a true devotee of the printed word, because she couldn't imagine submitting her work to such a disagreeable person. "I wouldn't be so quick to assume that," she said. "Publishing is a subjective business. Avis Roth is merely one opinion."

"But a highly regarded one." Ducking his head in dejection, Eban stubbed the toe of his boot against the tile. "She's put many authors on the best-seller list, including Oren Edwards, who I heard is staying here this week."

"He is indeed." Faith smiled at the reminder. Oren Edwards was considered the F. Scott Fitzgerald of his generation. It was very fitting that he would be one of the featured speakers during Gatsby Week. The retreat would officially begin tomorrow, but booklovers, scholars, and literary professionals, anxious to celebrate the works of Fitzgerald, were already flocking to Castleton Manor.

And that thought brought something else to mind. Before heading to the library, she needed to change out of her modern clothing and into one of the 1920s frocks she'd been provided. Under the direction of Charlotte Jaxon, who co-owned the manor along with her sons, most staff members were to wear period garb during the week. Judging by Eban's jeans and work boots, he was one of the exceptions.

"Please excuse me. I've got to get going." Faith picked up her coffee cup and the plate holding a cold English muffin. She'd have to eat it that way. There was no time to make a new one.

Eban shook himself out of a glum reverie. "I'd better get to work too. I'll have the trimming done before lunch."

"Thanks. See you later." Faith flew into the house, deftly avoiding Watson, who tried to run through her legs. "Fitz is gone, so there's no point in going out there," she told the sulky cat. "You can come to work with me if you behave yourself."

Faith glanced out the open window toward the garden, where Eban was wielding clippers. What must people think when they heard her talking to her cat?

Fifteen minutes later, Faith left the cottage, dressed in a pink-striped frock that grazed her knees, feeling both shapeless and free in the dropped-waist silhouette. She wore strappy sandals, and a cloche hat sat on her pinned-up chestnut locks.

Watson, trotting beside her, glanced up now and then as if not quite sure he recognized his mistress.

They hurried through the ornate gardens, careful not to get drenched by the automatic sprinklers. Even this early in the day, the sky had the white haze that foretold another scorcher. Scents of grass and flowers filled the salt-tinged air, and the sound of lazy breakers hitting the beach mingled with birdsong.

Castleton Manor stood like an empress on a slight rise, a delightfully incongruous three-story French Renaissance mansion near the small town of Lighthouse Bay, Massachusetts. Built in 1895, the château was a beautiful example of Gilded Age excess.

Faith adored every nook and cranny of the building, and as she and Watson entered the echoing Main Hall and passed through the magnificent Great Hall Gallery, she paused to admire the statue of Dame Agatha Christie. What a great way to start the day.

The same couldn't be said for finding Marlene Russell, the assistant manager, waiting by the library door. Marlene, smartly dressed in a period blue linen dress with short sleeves and a square white collar trimmed with lace, checked her dainty watch with a frown.

"I'm sorry I'm late," Faith said, rummaging for her key. Why Marlene hadn't unlocked the door herself was beyond her. The woman cherished her complete set of keys to the manor, although for once she didn't seem to be carrying them. "I was helping Ms. Roth. Fitz got away from her."

Marlene's pale green eyes widened. "What on earth are you talking about?"

Faith filled her in regarding the ferret incident as she unlocked the door, then stepped aside to let Marlene precede her into the room.

Watson didn't observe protocol, and he managed to slip past Marlene and enter the room first.

"Ms. Roth is staying in Wolfe's apartment with Charlotte, along with Oren and Lorraine Edwards and Hildegarde Maxwell," Marlene said. "I hope you didn't upset her. The last thing I need is a complaint from Charlotte."

Charlotte Jaxon had founded the book retreat, but since her oldest son, Wolfe, held the reins, she was rarely in residence. And when she was, Marlene, always a perfectionist, became even more demanding and finicky. The staff liked the gracious and charming Charlotte, but they dreaded the effect of her arrival on their boss.

"Ms. Roth is fine," Faith said, forcing a soothing tone into her voice. She set her tote on her desk, a lovely carved piece like all the manor's furnishings. "And so is her ferret."

Marlene gave a snort but didn't comment further. "I wanted to discuss the schedule with you before things get into full swing tomorrow." She moved toward an armchair, only to again be beaten to the punch by Watson.

Faith's exclamation saved the manager from sitting right on top of the cat.

Marlene shooed him away. "Must you always get in the way?"

Watson blinked at Marlene as if to say, "Yes, I must." He gave a loud, racketing purr and rubbed against her ankles.

"He likes you," Faith said, a reassurance she made frequently, hoping that Marlene would relent and allow herself to befriend the cat in return.

The library door flew open, and Brooke Milner, Faith's friend, raced in. "Faith, I've been waiting for you to show up." She spotted Marlene and came to a skidding halt. "Oh, I didn't know you were in a meeting."

"What is it?" Marlene gazed down her imperious nose at the sous-chef. "Is there an emergency in the kitchen?"

Brooke pushed a hand through her short blonde hair, which looked wonderfully appropriate with her blue-and-white striped dress and bib apron from the Jazz Age. "No, not that I know of. I was doing some research online about meals of the 1920s, and I found the Waldorf Astoria's signature red velvet cake recipe. I was hoping to locate other period recipes in the library."

Marlene's face crinkled in a frown. "Red cake? Surely not."

"I love red velvet cake," Faith said. "With cream cheese frosting, right? I might have something that will help you, Brooke. The other day I found a handwritten recipe book from one of Castleton's cooks. She worked here from 1920 until 1945." She smiled at Marlene. "It will only take me a minute to get it for her."

Marlene made a gesture of resigned disgust. Then, in an unprecedented display of playfulness, she tapped her shoe on the carpet to attract Watson's attention.

Not one to miss an opportunity, the cat pounced, landing on the rug when she moved her foot. And on it went.

Brooke followed Faith to the cookbook section. "I have someone I want you to meet." She gave Faith a significant smile.

Faith shook her head. "Don't tell me. Another one of your dates." Brooke had an active, frequently disastrous dating life. But she was good-humored about it and often shared cringeworthy anecdotes during the book club meetings she and Faith attended.

"No, this is even better. My cousin Taylor Milner is staying at Castleton this week. She's Avis Roth's literary assistant."

"Your cousin is in town? I can't wait to meet her." Faith knew that family meant a lot to Brooke. The young sous-chef had spent the early years of her childhood in foster care before being adopted into the Milner clan, a tight-knit, loving family.

"I'll bring her to the book club tonight." They met at the Candle House Library in town, joined by Eileen Piper, Candle House's head librarian and Faith's aunt, and Midge Foster, the concierge veterinarian for Castleton Manor.

"That's a great idea. Eileen and Midge will want to meet her too." Faith found the cookbook and slid it from its spot. The manor library had thousands of volumes, and they were organized using a standard library system. It made her job much easier. "Here you go." She handed the book to her friend. "I hope you find some inspiration."

Brooke leafed through it. "This is fabulous. There's even a section with menus for house parties and events." She held the book aloft. "Score."

Faith smiled at Brooke's infectious enthusiasm, enjoying the satisfaction of connecting another library patron to the knowledge she sought.

"I'd better get back to Marlene," Faith said, noticing that the manager was still playing with Watson. *Wonders will never cease.* Marlene had always made it clear that she wasn't fond of animals, despite Castleton Manor's pet-friendly policy.

"Not just Marlene." Brooke lowered her voice. "Here comes Wolfe."

The bachelor millionaire and manor owner strolled into the library, looking handsome in a period men's suit complete with a newsboy cap. Wolfe's blue eyes lit up when he spotted Faith. "I've been looking for you."

Behind his back, Brooke gave a subtle thumbs-up. No matter how often Faith asserted that Wolfe was not interested in her romantically, Brooke refused to believe it. Then she slipped out of the room.

"This is the place to find her," Marlene said. "We were getting ready to discuss this week's activities."

Wolfe tore his gaze away from Faith. "I'm glad you're here, Marlene. I want to make a slight adjustment to our plans."

Marlene straightened. "Oh? What's that?"

"My mother wants Faith to be her assistant this week." Wolfe shrugged. "I know it's not librarian work, but it'd be most appreciated. That is, if you can spare her."

Asking Marlene was a wise move. And as Faith expected, the manager readily agreed, almost smiling in the process. "Of course. Whatever Mrs. Jaxon needs, we're happy to provide."

Wolfe gave a decisive nod. "Good. Now that's settled, Mother would like to see you upstairs in my office right away, Faith. Go ahead. The door's open."

A few minutes later, Faith, with Watson trailing, entered the third-floor apartment that was the Jaxon domain. Usually Wolfe lived up here alone, but with more than half a dozen bedrooms, two living rooms, a family library, and various other rooms, he and his mother could coexist for weeks without bumping into each other. Additional guests were easily accommodated.

As she crossed the living room to Wolfe's office, her shoes sinking into the deep carpet, the door to the library burst open.

A man stormed out, yelling over his shoulder, "You'll regret this, Avis. Just you wait and see!"

Faith stopped dead, startled by the stranger's appearance. Looking more closely at him as he charged her way, head down, arms swinging, she recognized Oren Edwards, the famous writer. Dressed in a Hawaiian shirt and jeans, he was of middle height and weight, with curly gray hair and a square jaw.

Oren faltered when he noticed Faith. Then he leveled a glare at her and marched past without saying a word.

As for Faith, she hurried the rest of the way to the office, pretending she hadn't seen or heard anything.

Charlotte Jaxon appeared in the office doorway, her fine-boned face breaking into a huge smile at the sight of Faith. In that expression, Faith saw her charming, personable sons, especially Wolfe. With her dark hair pulled back and dressed in a pink floral chiffon frock, Charlotte was effortlessly elegant.

"Faith, my dear. How good of you to agree to my request." Charlotte clasped Faith's hand with cool fingers. She noticed Watson standing with face upturned. "And you too, Watson, you handsome creature." She crouched and petted him thoroughly.

Watson purred loudly.

"Sorry," Charlotte said with a laugh. "I don't have cats anymore, so I have to take my feline fix where I can."

"He doesn't mind," Faith said. Between Marlene and Charlotte, Watson was getting the spoiling of his life. And it wasn't even noon yet.

Charlotte put her arm through Faith's and guided her in the other direction, Watson following. "I could use another cup of coffee, so let's talk in the kitchen." As they passed the library, the older woman indicated the doorway. "Avis Roth is working in there." Charlotte lowered her voice. "She's quite formidable, but don't be fooled. Her bark is worse than her bite."

I wonder if Oren Edwards agrees. Faith turned her attention fully to Charlotte, who was detailing the jam-packed schedule of events. In addition to the lectures and gatherings that were a retreat's usual fare, there would be events at the Lighthouse Bay Country Club and even a series of antique car races at Blake Jaxon's track in New Hampshire.

"I'll be behind the wheel of a 1925 Bentley convertible," Charlotte announced.

"How exciting." Faith added this knowledge to what little she knew of Charlotte. But she wasn't surprised. Her sons were bold, adventurous, and full of life. They must have gotten it from their mother. And perhaps her late husband, Henry, who had died almost a decade ago. He'd been quite a businessman, and Wolfe had inherited his empire.

Charlotte winked at Faith. "You didn't know I was a hotshot race car driver, did you?"

The cat slipped into the library, having detected the odor of the interesting creature from earlier. Two humans were seated at a long table. The one he'd met before frowned at the other, who was younger.

"I'm going to have to let Oren go," the older one said. "His sales are tanking."

"But maybe the new book will—"

"Who's the expert here? The one with a few dozen best sellers under her belt? Or you, barely out of college and from the boondocks of Massachusetts?"

He didn't like that human. He could tell she was the kind that would kick him if he attracted her attention. He slipped out of view under the table, sniffing to find his friend. Ah, there he was. The poor thing was locked in a cage. The cat went up to say hello.

The ferret chattered and moved closer, stretching out his nose.

"What's the matter with Fitz? Oh, it's that cat again. Go on. Get out of here."

Faith and Charlotte reached the kitchen, where Charlotte proceeded to make coffee. "Have a seat," she said, pointing to the barstools at one end of the granite counter.

Faith set down her tote and perched on a stool. "Thanks for providing the period clothes. It's really fun to dress up." The outfits delivered to her cottage had been accompanied by a note from Charlotte.

Wolfe's mother shrugged. "I know it's a bit over the top, but I thought it would be interesting. Perhaps dressing like people of the period will help us understand them better."

"Then I'm glad we aren't studying the Victorian era," Faith said with a laugh. She put a hand to her midriff. "I'd hate to be wearing a corset right now. Or a hoop skirt."

Charlotte pulled at her dress, demonstrating how loose it was around the waist. "I hear you. Getting rid of corsets must have felt like heaven for the women of a hundred years ago."

"And clothes of the 1920s now seem constraining and formal to us, especially hats and gloves." Faith smoothed her skirt. "But I have to say, wearing this makes me wish we dressed up every day."

"Exactly. My usual summer morning outfit is capris and a T-shirt." Charlotte held out a tanned leg. "I did take the liberty of not wearing stockings. I couldn't stand them in this heat." She opened a cupboard and selected a couple of mugs. "Do you take cream and sugar?"

"Milk, please. No sugar." The aroma of high-quality coffee filled the air, and Faith inhaled it with appreciation.

Watson galloped into the kitchen. He paused to look around, then leaped up onto the stool next to Faith.

"Where have you been, Rumpy?" She smoothed his ruffled fur. Something must have spooked him.

"Is that fresh java I smell?" A woman appeared in the doorway. Around Charlotte's age, she was also dressed in a flowing chiffon dress. Her graying blonde hair hung loose, and she'd tucked a blossom over her ear.

"Lorraine, this is Faith Newberry, our delightful librarian here at Castleton." Charlotte poured steaming coffee into the cups. "Faith, this is Lorraine Edwards."

Oren's wife. Faith smiled and said hello.

Lorraine waved a hand in greeting and drifted over to stand near Charlotte. "Oren is in a real snit." She leaned against the counter and crossed her arms.

"When isn't he?" Charlotte said lightly. She opened the cupboard again and retrieved another mug. "Writers are temperamental, you know."

Lorraine sighed. "I suppose. He's such a bear to live with when he gets this way."

She seemed to either forget Faith was there or dismiss her presence, something Faith had noticed among certain wealthy people. If you were in the category of "help," you were presumed both deaf and blind.

"He's irate about Avis's opinion of his new book." Lorraine gave a tinkling laugh. "He said he almost leaped across the table and strangled her when she critiqued it."

"Sometimes I just want to strangle her." The young woman Faith assumed was Taylor Milner rolled her big blue eyes. "Have you ever had a boss who drove you crazy?" Brooke's cousin was cute, with creamy skin and blonde hair. She wore hot pink flip-flops, a white denim skirt, and a pink T-shirt. Adorably dorky horn-rimmed glasses perched on her nose.

"I think it's required of bosses to be annoying," Brooke replied. Then she noticed Faith's arrival at the Candle House Library and smiled at her. "They finally let you out of the salt mines?"

With a sigh, Faith plopped into the chair next to them. "Yes, finally. I thought it would be a cakewalk working with Charlotte, but she's even more demanding than Marlene. I'm exhausted."

Watson, who had accompanied her, gave a huge yawn and stretch, as though to underscore Faith's words.

The other two laughed.

"What a sweet cat," Taylor said.

"As you probably already guessed," Brooke said, "this is Taylor, my cousin."

"It's great to meet you." Faith shook Taylor's hand, noticing that she had a much more assertive grip than her boss. She looked around for the other members. "Where is everyone?"

"Eileen is still in her office, and Midge hasn't arrived yet." Brooke reached for the hardcover book sitting on an end table beside her. The club had been reading Luis Gerardo's latest novel over the past couple of weeks. She flipped the book around to show the photograph of the author. "Get this. Taylor knows Luis Gerardo. *Personally.*"

"He's arriving at Castleton tomorrow to be part of Gatsby Week." Faith studied the author photo, which displayed a handsome young man with dark hair and an infectious grin. "He looks like a nice guy. And he's incredibly talented. I'm really enjoying his book."

Taylor's cheeks pinked. She took Luis's novel and studied the photo, touching it with gentle fingers. "He's wonderful." She lowered her voice. "Avis actually turned him down. He went to another agency, and now he's a best-selling author."

"She must hate that," Brooke said. "The one that got away."

"How did you meet Luis?" Faith asked. "When he was submitting to Avis?"

"At a publishing conference." The assistant's lips tightened. "Aspiring authors aren't allowed anywhere near our office. Avis hates it when they dare to speak to her."

"I witnessed that in person," Faith said. "Eban Matthews had his head handed to him this morning." She explained the sequence of events that had occurred at the cottage.

"Eban wrote a book?" Brooke asked. "I didn't know that."

"It's about a climbing tragedy in the White Mountains," Faith responded. "He said it's based on a true story."

"Eban's really good," Taylor said. "I read his submission and recommended he join our agency. But Avis rejected him. I don't understand why. I thought his manuscript was a winner."

Faith's aunt bustled out of her office. In her early sixties, Eileen was trim and attractive, with sparkling blue eyes and an energetic manner. "Sorry I'm late. I had an order I needed to submit today, and the Internet was acting up." She smiled at Taylor. "I see we have a new addition to the club."

Brooke introduced her cousin to Eileen and then to Midge, who arrived just then with Atticus, her Chihuahua. As always, he wore his Doggles, special glasses for his failing eyesight.

The women exclaimed over the dog's cuteness while Watson looked on with disdain.

"It's neat that you guys bring your pets everywhere," Taylor said. "Maybe I should have brought Fitz."

"Fitz is her boss's ferret," Faith explained to the others. "He's so cute."

"Would you like to meet a ferret?" Midge cooed to Atticus. "I wonder if the two of them would get along." She put her ear next to the dog's mouth, then shook her head. "He says no."

Faith and Eileen exchanged amused glances. In their view, Atticus hadn't said a thing.

"I thought Kate was coming tonight," Eileen said to Midge.

Midge's daughter, Kate, was home for the summer while applying to master's degree programs in marine biology.

"She'll be here in a few. She got hung up at work," Midge said. "Kate is waiting tables at the country club. She says the tips are fantastic."

"I've heard that," Brooke said. "The food is good there too, which always helps the tips."

"I'll be experiencing the food for myself," Faith said. "Charlotte has planned several activities at the club this week."

"She's having us wear 1920s clothing," Brooke added. "I don't mind, but it felt good to put on shorts and a T-shirt tonight."

"Women's clothing had a lot of social meaning in the 1920s." Eileen cracked open her copy of Luis's book. "I noticed that clothes seemed to hold the same symbolism in this book, which many reviewers compared to *The Great Gatsby.*"

"What a great observation." Taylor tapped the book she held. "Luis made the point that brands are used to peg people's social status and aspirations."

With Taylor's remark, a clamorous discussion was launched, with everyone chiming in with thoughts and observations.

A voice cut through the noise. "Wow. Who knew the book group was so lively?"

They all turned to take in a tall young woman with long, curly brown hair and hazel eyes.

"Kate, you made it." Still holding Atticus, Midge jumped up to give her daughter a peck on the cheek. "How was work?"

Kate burst into tears. "Mom, someone stole Grandma's earrings."

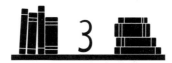

The group broke into exclamations of dismay.

Midge took her daughter's arm. "Come sit down and tell us what happened."

Kate's face screwed up in distress. "You're not mad?" As she sat next to her mother, she said, "I know you told me not to wear them to work."

"I'm more concerned about you than a pair of earrings." Midge set Atticus down and foraged for a pack of tissues in her purse, which she handed to Kate. "How about a glass of iced tea and a cookie?"

"I'll get them." Eileen rose and went to the refreshment table.

"Can you please bring me another one of your lemon cookies?" Brooke called.

Eileen smiled over her shoulder. "I'll bring the plate over. How's that?" She offered the plate to Midge and gave Kate a glass of tea and a napkin.

Midge let Kate take a cookie, then passed the plate to Brooke.

After everyone was settled and Kate had met Taylor, Midge said, "Tell us what happened."

Kate sniffed. "Things have been disappearing at the country club lately. At first we assumed people were just misplacing things, but after the third or fourth time, the waitstaff started to think someone is stealing."

"What kind of things have gone missing?" Faith asked.

"A digital camera, a gold lighter sitting on the bar, leather driving gloves, and a pair of expensive sunglasses. And now my earrings."

"Where were the earrings?" Midge asked. "Did they maybe fall off?"

Kate shook her head. "I lost the back to one, so I put them in my purse, which was in my locker. Tonight when I went to leave, they were gone but my money and cards were still in my wallet."

"Are you sure you put them in there?" At her daughter's impatient assurance, Midge said, "Then someone broke into your locker. You need to tell the manager."

"I will. He wasn't in tonight."

"What do they look like? I'll keep my eyes peeled in case the thief decides to wear them." Brooke tapped her earlobes in demonstration.

"They were opals surrounded by diamonds. Not huge but really pretty." Another tear trickled down Kate's face. "I hope we find them."

"We'll check the pawnshops," Faith suggested. "You never know, the thief might be dumb enough to get rid of them right here in town."

"And report the loss to the police," Eileen said. "They'll put the item on a list they circulate."

Taylor regarded the women with astonishment. "You sound like investigators. I'm impressed."

The others burst into laughter.

Brooke patted her cousin on the arm. "Do I have some stories to share with you!"

Somehow they never made it back to the book discussion the rest of the meeting. Faith enjoyed the general discussion, feeling like she was better acquainted with both Taylor and Kate by evening's end.

Mindful of an early morning, Faith and Watson headed home around nine thirty, driving through the quiet streets of Lighthouse Bay.

While at one of the few traffic lights, a couple loitering in front of McGinty's Irish pub caught Faith's eye. *Is that Luis Gerardo? But he's not due in town until tomorrow.*

The young woman he was speaking with was petite, with cropped brown hair. She definitely wasn't Taylor. Faith's belly clenched. At the meeting, Faith had gotten the impression that Luis and Taylor were involved romantically or that Taylor had feelings for him at least. While she watched, Luis and the woman walked away, laughing together.

None of my business, right? The light changed, and Faith hit the gas, leaving them—and her speculations—behind.

Faith steered down the private drive at Castleton Manor, parked her SUV at the cottage, and walked to the door with Watson. The breeze was soft, and crickets chirped in the grass. Overhead, stars twinkled gently.

A figure moved in the shadows next to the house, making Faith jump.

"Sorry. I didn't mean to startle you." Wolfe rose from the bench near the door. "I came over to see if you were home, then sat here for a while enjoying the evening."

"No problem." Faith glanced down at Watson, who was rubbing against Wolfe's legs. "If you were a stranger, he would have reacted much differently." She laughed. "Think hissing and scratching."

"Are you a watch kitty?" Wolfe crouched to scratch Watson under the chin.

Faith unlocked the door. "Would you like to come in? I could use a glass of iced tea."

"I'd love to." Wolfe tugged at the collar of his shirt. "It's a hot and humid one for sure. And more of this weather to come this week."

"That's good for the conference, right?" Faith flicked on lights as she went through the cottage. "I understand from your mother there's a lot of golf in our future. And car races. Can't do that in the rain."

Wolfe settled at the kitchen table at her gesture. "That's what I want to talk to you about."

"The race?" Faith reached for two tall glasses and set them on the counter. "You won't catch me in one of those cars," she joked.

He sighed. "Not exactly. I'll wait until you sit down."

"That sounds ominous." She hurried to put ice cubes in the glasses and fill them with iced tea from the refrigerator. Then a plate of lemon slices, long spoons, the sugar bowl, and napkins. Last she opened the back door to let in the breeze and cracked the window above the sink.

After Wolfe doctored his tea with a little sugar and a lemon slice, he said, "There's no easy way to say this. I'm worried about Mother."

"What's wrong?" A parent having problems was scary business indeed. And she liked Charlotte very much.

He shook his head. "She'd say nothing, but I beg to differ. You see, the doctor just put her on blood pressure medicine. But do you think that would slow her down? Oh no, not Charlotte Jaxon. She's still go, go, go."

Faith thought back to her day with Charlotte. They'd spent the hours in a whirl of planning, making calls, double-checking arrangements, and touring the manor to set up for the conference. The older woman had far outpaced her, bouncing from one thing to another. "I can't argue with you there."

Wolfe stirred his tea with a clink of cubes, then tapped the spoon and set it on a napkin. "So you see what I'm talking about? She needs to take it easy."

A creeping suspicion swept over Faith. "And you think I can help with that?" She heard the doubt in her rising tone. "I couldn't possibly . . ." What was that saying about fools rushing in?

"I know full well how stubborn my mother can be. Even bullheaded." His eyes twinkled. "I take after her, right? I'm asking you to keep an eye on her, and if it seems like she's overdoing it, tell her *you* need a break. She's a thoughtful woman, so she'll slow down for you."

Laughter bubbled up in Faith's chest. "You want me to pretend I'm the one who needs to move at a snail's pace. I can do that." She grinned. "Besides, it's true. I'm exhausted from trying to keep up, and it's only been one day."

"I knew I could count on you. I really appreciate it." Wolfe took a long drink of iced tea. "This is really hitting the spot."

"Are you hungry? I made molasses cookies the other day." Faith hopped up and grabbed the tin.

Someone knocked on the front door.

"Excuse me," she told Wolfe, setting the cookies on the table.

Wolfe swiveled around in his seat. "I didn't know you were expecting a visitor." Did Faith detect a note of affronted surprise in his voice?

"I wasn't," she said, then hurried to answer the door.

Eban stood there, holding a manila envelope. "I came by earlier, but you weren't home," the gardener said. "Then I saw the lights and thought I'd give it a shot."

"Please come in." Faith led him to the kitchen.

When Eban saw Wolfe, he shifted his feet awkwardly. "Hi, Mr. Jaxon. Sorry to barge in on you guys." He waved the envelope. "I was hoping you could read this for me, Faith."

Wolfe's face lightened—at hearing Eban's reason for visiting, perhaps? "I need to get going anyway." He pushed back from the table and stood, then carried his used glass and spoon to the sink.

Faith tried to hide her disappointment as she said goodbye to Wolfe and invited Eban to sit at the table. "Iced tea? Cookies?"

Eban said yes to both, munching and sipping away while Faith refilled her own glass of tea.

Faith sat down. "So what's up?" She checked the wall clock, hoping he wouldn't be long-winded.

Eban tapped the envelope. "This is a revised version of my novel. Since you're such a great librarian, I thought you'd be able to give me some good feedback." He looked at her expectantly.

What could she say? "I'll do my best. But I can't promise to get through the whole thing right away. I'm really busy with the conference." *And monitoring Charlotte's health.*

He gave a shout of joy. "If you can read the first few chapters, that would be amazing. Maybe I can give Ms. Roth the revised version in person later this week before she leaves."

Unease chimed in Faith's mind like a distant bell. "Are you sure that's such a good idea? She wasn't exactly nice this morning."

With a laugh, Eban leaned his chair back on two legs. "I know, right? But writers need to have tough skins. I moped around for part of the day, but then I decided to give it another shot. All she can do is say no." He brought the chair upright with a thump.

"I suppose so. I'll take a look over the next day or two." She glanced at the clock. "I hate to rush you, but . . ."

He jumped up, hitting the table and making it wobble. "Oops. Sorry. I'm a little clumsy when I get excited." He pushed his chair under the table. "I'll let you be." With a jaunty whistle, he exited through the front door.

Faith followed, then shut the door and locked it. "Ready for bed, Watson?"

Seven o'clock arrived much too early for Faith the next morning. Despite her resolution, she had stayed up until after midnight reading Eban's book. It was gripping, so well written that Faith felt like she was accompanying the climbing party as they ascended a steep, snow-covered trail up Mount Washington. She felt the icy wind in her face, the unstable ground shifting under her feet, the burn of aching muscles. And most vividly of all, a growing sense of impending doom.

The atmosphere of the book stayed with her as she showered and dressed and made her way to the manor. *Why did Avis reject Eban?* Even Faith, admittedly not well versed in the acquisitions side of publishing, could tell it was a superb book.

Too weary to trudge up two flights of stairs, Faith took the elevator to Wolfe's apartment, to Watson's chagrin. After she'd explained that Watson usually accompanied her to the library, Charlotte had graciously agreed that he could be a regular visitor to the apartment.

Faith let herself in as instructed. Charlotte had said to meet her in the dining room, so she traversed the corridors to the other end of the apartment, past the kitchen, her furry shadow close on her heels. As they drew close, the sounds of chatter and clinking dishes drifted Faith's way, as well as the aromas of coffee and bacon. Her stomach gurgling, she picked up her pace, eager for breakfast.

Then a shriek of dismay rang out, followed by the smash of china.

4

I*s Charlotte ill?* Faith bolted for the dining room, matched by a cantering cat. In the doorway, she jerked to a stop, using the doorjamb as a brake. She swiftly took in the scene.

Avis stood at the head of the table, clutching what appeared to be a letter. Oren bent near her feet, picking up pieces of china, while Lorraine fluttered around with napkins, mopping up the spill.

"Leave it," Charlotte said, sitting calmly at the other end of the table, fork poised over a plate of scrambled eggs. Thankfully, she appeared perfectly healthy. "The staff will take care of it. You'll cut yourself, Oren."

"Ouch." He put a finger to his mouth. "Too late."

Lorraine grabbed another napkin and wrapped it around his finger.

Avis, seeing their attention diverted, gave another shriek. "The absolute nerve of this person, threatening me!"

No one responded, and activity continued to go on around Avis—Faith entering the room and serving herself at the breakfast buffet and Oren and Lorraine muttering over his cut finger.

Avis shook the paper. "Listen to this. 'Dear Avis. While I find much to admire about your work, I regret to inform you that it doesn't meet my needs at this time. In fact, you have rejected your last author and soured your final publishing deal—'"

Watson, sitting at the agent's feet, gave the loud yowl Faith knew signified displeasure. She decided to listen more closely. Perhaps there was something to Avis's concerns.

Avis peered down at Watson. "You don't like it either, do you, cat? I might have to revise my opinion of you." She cackled. "This creature is smarter than all of you."

"What are you on about now, Avis?" A woman swished into the dining room, wrinkling her elegant nose in disdain. She wore her silver hair in a French twist and, like the other women, was dressed in an eyelet cotton summer frock.

The agent marched across the room. "I got another threatening letter today." She thrust it under the woman's nose. "Read that last line."

The newcomer scanned the page, lips moving. Then she read, "'This is my final warning.' Oh my, that does sound alarming." But her tone and the lift of her eyebrows said otherwise.

The others in the room laughed, except for Faith, who found the scrambled eggs had turned to ash in her mouth. She swallowed and said, "I hate to disagree, but I think we need to take that letter seriously."

Avis hooted with glee. "At last! Someone else who gets it. She's as smart as her cat." She whirled on the new arrival. "See, Hildegarde? Fiona thinks it's real."

"My name is Faith, and yes, I do think it's real. Mrs. Jaxon, I think we should call the police."

"You really think so?" Charlotte sounded doubtful. "It's obviously a disgruntled writer."

"Excuse me, but who are you?" Hildegarde said to Faith, folding her arms across her chest. "We haven't been introduced."

Charlotte waved a hand. "Hildegarde, meet Faith Newberry, our wonderful librarian. Faith, this is Hildegarde Maxwell, my dear friend. Her husband was Francis Maxwell, the famous editor."

Oren, standing by the coffee maker, drawled, "He's the man who plucked me from obscurity. And as they say, the rest is history."

Avis snorted. "Yes, *history* is the correct word. Oh, and get me another coffee, will you?" She plopped down in her chair.

The author shot Avis a glare, then resumed filling his cup. Lorraine fluttered to his side, and once again the couple held a whispered conversation. Oren didn't pour Avis a cup, Faith noticed, but Lorraine did, then served it to the agent.

Avis took it without thanks, doctoring it with cream and sugar.

Hildegarde filled a plate and sat beside Faith. "What's on the agenda for today, Charlotte?"

"There's not much going on this morning, but this afternoon there's a tea at the country club. Oren is scheduled to give a talk."

"After I play a round of golf," the author said, glancing at his gold watch. He studied his finger, still swaddled in a napkin. "I hope I can swing straight with this injury. In any case, I'd better go finish my notes so I can make my tee time." Carrying his coffee, he left the room.

Lorraine settled across from Faith with her own cup.

"Hey, people." Avis flapped her hand. "Let's not forget my problem."

Hildegarde eyed her up and down. "Which problem is that?"

"My threatening letter." She slapped her hand on the table. "It was delivered here, to Castleton. That means my stalker knows where I am."

Charlotte knit her brow. "That's the problem nowadays. With social media, people can easily track someone down."

"I don't use social media," Avis said. "For that very reason. Otherwise I'd have wannabes accosting me everywhere."

So it's someone who knows her schedule. An insider. Faith tucked away that insight. "I think to be on the safe side, we should call the police. I know the local officers well. Shall I place the call?"

Charlotte nodded. "If you think we should, then I'll bow to your judgment."

"I'll do it right after breakfast." Faith picked up a piece of toast, forcing herself to eat for sustenance for the day ahead.

"Nana, I was hoping to find you here." A young woman breezed in and bent to kiss Hildegarde's cheek.

With a start, Faith recognized the woman she had seen with Luis Gerardo the night before.

"Ivy," Charlotte said, "how nice to see you. Have a seat."

Ivy shook her head. "Thanks, but I can't. I have to head out to the country club. I'm working today."

"But you're still on for our concert tonight?" Charlotte asked. "Ivy has the most gorgeous singing voice," she told the others. "She reminds me of a modern-day Peggy Lee."

The young woman blushed, fidgeting with the many rings on her fingers. "I don't know about that. But I'm looking forward to singing with Luis."

Faith felt a pang of relief on Taylor's behalf. Maybe the connection between Luis and Ivy was purely professional.

Lorraine fanned her hand in front of her face. "Luis Gerardo. What a doll." Her glance at Avis was sly. "And the best writer of his generation."

Avis harrumphed, pretending great interest in her beverage. "Publishing hype."

"I've got to dash. See you later." Ivy hoisted her bag to a more secure position on her shoulder and slipped out of the room.

"Luis was one of my students at the Bradley School in New York City," Lorraine said to Faith. "His mother was a teacher too. Weren't you a trustee then, Avis?"

"I was until I decided I'd better cut back on my volunteer work," the agent said. "That will suck the life out of you if you're not careful."

Charlotte, who did a great deal of charity work, pursed her lips but didn't comment. Instead, she turned to Faith. "Shall we go to the office? I want to discuss a few things with you." She picked up her cup. "Let's bring our coffee." She smiled at the cat behind her. "And Watson."

"Don't forget to call the cops," Avis said. "I'll be in the library with my evidence."

After they settled at a round table in the office, Watson in the window seat grooming, Faith pulled out her phone to call the police. Before she dialed, she sent Eban a quick text to tell him he had her thumbs-up on his manuscript.

He immediately responded with enthusiastic thanks.

"You could use the house phone," Charlotte said, flipping her conference binder open.

"Thanks, but I have the police station number already logged." What that said about Faith's life, she didn't care to contemplate.

The dispatcher put her straight through to Chief Andy Garris, who happened to be in the office. After a brief chat, she disconnected. "He'll be over shortly to take a look at the note."

Charlotte took off her reading glasses and swung them by the bow. "You really think Avis is in danger?"

Before Faith could answer, someone rapped on the door, and a second later, Wolfe walked in. "Mind if I join you?"

"Of course not." Charlotte smiled at her son. "Have a seat."

"Morning, Faith." Wolfe nodded to her as he pulled out a chair. "How are things going with the event?"

"Great. We're getting ready to go over today's schedule." Faith opened her own copy of the binder.

"After we deal with the police," Charlotte said. She explained the situation regarding Avis's anonymous letter.

"Better safe than sorry, I suppose." Wolfe shook his head. "Mother, I hate to say this, but Avis is a lightning rod for drama. There's always something going on with her, and it's never pleasant."

Charlotte laughed. "*Drama?* You're right, but I never thought I'd hear you say that."

He shrugged. "In this case, it's the perfect description. Why do you keep her around?"

Faith, fascinated by this frank dialogue between mother and son, waited for Charlotte's answer.

She took her time formulating a response, shoving her glasses into her hair and fiddling with a pen. "She reminds me of the unpopular kid who keeps drawing attention to herself in obnoxious ways but never understands why it's not helping."

Ouch. Faith cringed. She hoped Charlotte would never offer an honest assessment of Faith's flaws.

Charlotte made a helpless gesture. "You might not remember this, but her brother was a very dear friend of your father's. It's to honor that friendship that I welcome Avis here."

Wolfe pressed his lips together. "Well, now I feel about an inch high. Your common decency humbles me."

"Oh, pshaw. You're a good man, Wolfe Jaxon." Charlotte turned to Faith. "Isn't he?"

"Oh yes," Faith mumbled, feeling her cheeks heat up at being put on the spot.

Wolfe regarded Faith with warm amusement, then rose from the table. "I'll let you ladies get back to work. You're at the country club this afternoon, right?"

"We are. You should join us for Oren's talk," Charlotte said. "It's going to be excellent."

"I'll try, but I have several calls to make first." Wolfe rested his hands on the back of the chair. "I'm trying to get things cleared up so I can spend the week enjoying the conference." He smiled at Faith. "You'll have to save me a dance at the Gatsby Ball." With that exciting promise, he left.

Faith and Charlotte spent a couple of hours going over the schedule and checking the roster of conference attendees. With Charlotte dictating, Faith sent them all a welcome e-mail with the latest agenda.

When Faith returned Watson to the cottage for the afternoon, he made sure Faith knew exactly how much he disapproved of the arrangement.

Then Charlotte ordered her car, and they left for the Lighthouse Bay Country Club. Faith had only driven past the wrought iron gates of the venerable club, founded in 1906. In Charlotte's car, they swept up a curving drive lined with ornamental trees. Here and there she glimpsed the golf greens, swaths of emerald green dotted with sand traps. Golfers strolled on foot or buzzed around in carts.

The clubhouse itself was a huge shingled cottage with dormers and a porch that circled three sides. Charlotte's driver pulled up into the portico to let them out, and a valet wearing a bow tie hurried over.

"I love this place," Charlotte said as she slid out, the valet reaching to assist her. "They have first-class service."

Faith was glad she was wearing a pretty dress and sandals, although the other guests were mostly casually dressed, albeit in designer labels. Such an imposing establishment quietly demanded a certain formality and sophistication.

"Charlotte Jaxon, how nice to see you." A short, slight man with a bald head, a beaky nose, and a high-pitched voice beetled over to greet them. He took Charlotte's hand, eyeing Faith curiously.

Charlotte tugged Faith forward. "Marvin Treadwell, this is Faith Newberry, our librarian. Marvin is the club manager. How many years have you been here, Marvin? I forget."

Marvin chuckled. "Too many to count, dear lady. But put it this way: your fine sons were junior golfers." He gestured for them to precede him. "I've put your group in the private dining room."

This sizable room, adjacent to the main dining room and overlooking the golf course, was lined with windows like a sunporch. On one wall was a buffet laden with silver chafing dishes and icy jugs of beverages. A podium was set up in the back of the room, and facing it were two long tables arranged in a T. Colorful flower arrangements marched down the center of the tables, and the linen cloths were snowy white, set off by dark green napkins with the club's crest.

Charlotte clasped her hands together in pleasure. "This is perfect. Thank you, Marvin."

The manager accepted her approval with a nod. "Kate and Ivy will be right in to assist you."

Voices were heard in the hall, and Avis and Hildegarde glided in, trailed by Taylor.

Avis stopped and planted her hands on her hips, taking in every detail. "Not bad. Although I would have gone with a different color palette."

Marvin and Charlotte exchanged amused looks.

"I'll leave you, ladies," the manager said. "Have a good meeting."

"How's it going, Faith?" Taylor appeared at her elbow.

Faith glanced around the room, which was rapidly filling with chattering men and women, most of them dressed in period clothing. "I think it's going great. It looks like we're getting a nice turnout."

"That's good news." Taylor pulled out a chair. "Mind if I sit next to you? I need to put a little distance between me and my boss for a while."

Smiling in reply, Faith also sat.

Charlotte was at the perpendicular head table with Avis and Hildegarde, the trio engaged in an animated discussion.

Dressed in a green skirt and a white shirt, Kate came around with a pitcher of water, pausing to say hello.

Taylor nudged Faith as she looked out the window. "Isn't Ivy supposed to be in here helping Kate?"

Faith followed her gaze. Ivy was talking to Eban, who wore an old-fashioned golfing outfit complete with knickers and a cap. *So she knows Eban too?* Ivy certainly seemed to be popular. "I would think so."

"You know, Eban would look great on a dust jacket," Taylor remarked.

Faith laughed. "So that's the secret of becoming a famous author. Being photogenic."

Taylor pursed her lips. "No, of course not. But it sure doesn't hurt the publicity campaign."

"I agree with you that Eban's manuscript is a winner," Faith said. "I started reading it last night, and I became so engrossed that I stayed up way too late. It's excellent."

"That's great to hear." Someone entering caught her eye, and Taylor waved with a smile. "There's one of our agency stars now."

Oren, accompanied by his wife, went to the head table to sit.

A server came with a cart and filled the chafing dishes while Kate continued to pour drinks, gradually herding everyone to their seats.

A windblown Ivy finally entered the room and conferred with an obviously annoyed Kate, who then went to Charlotte and whispered something.

Charlotte tapped her glass with a knife a few times. After the crowd quieted, she stood to welcome everyone and issued an invitation to line up for the buffet.

Faith and Charlotte hung back until the last, but the rest of the group had no such compunction as they swarmed the food line.

Faith returned to her seat with a plate containing the tiniest piece of chicken she'd ever seen and a spoonful of scalloped potatoes. The salad was down to a few lettuce leaves and a lone cherry tomato.

Taylor was already eating. "This is so good." She sliced a fat shrimp in two. "You didn't get any shrimp?"

"No, it was all gone." Faith shook out her napkin and placed it on her lap. She picked up her fork and knife. "That's okay. I'm not really hungry." Her belly rumbled, contradicting her words. She reached for a roll. Bread would have to suffice until she got home.

After the diners were more or less finished, Charlotte tapped on her glass again. "I hope you enjoyed your meal. Let's give our servers a hand."

The group obediently clapped for Kate and Ivy.

"They'll be bringing around coffee and dessert while we listen to our wonderful speaker. Please welcome one of America's finest novelists, Oren Edwards."

The audience erupted in cheers and applause.

Oren rose from his seat, shedding his napkin and straightening his watch. He moved to the podium. "I'm excited to be with you all in this historic country club, built in the same style that Fitzgerald would have enjoyed." With that introduction, he launched into his lecture, "Class and Social Status in F. Scott Fitzgerald's Fiction—and Beyond."

Faith found his talk fascinating. Oren discussed how aspirations provided a framework for Fitzgerald's plots—and his own. Other themes included the discovery that such material desires held more gilt than gold, and true love was more valuable than any worldly status.

Taylor sighed at points, her eyes gleaming. "He's so right," she whispered to Faith. "Love is so much more important than money, isn't it?"

"If I had to choose, that's what I'd pick," Faith whispered back.

Oren wrapped up soon after to another round of applause, then sat down to eat chocolate cake with his wife, his agent, and his hostess.

Others in the room approached him, lugging volumes of his latest novel for him to autograph, and the session became an impromptu book signing.

After the attendees finally cleared out, Charlotte and her group got ready to return to the manor. With a dinner scheduled that evening at Castleton, the rest of the afternoon was free.

"Are you going back out on the golf course this afternoon?" Hildegarde asked Oren.

Oren dabbed his forehead with a handkerchief and tucked it away. "Not today. I already got a little too much sun." He felt at his wrist, frowning. "Where did I put my watch?" He searched around his seat, then walked to the podium. "Has anyone seen my watch?" His frown deepened to a scowl. "My gold watch is gone."

5

The ladies fluttered around Oren with exclamations of dismay, looking under the table and on the floor.

"Did you leave it in the locker room after your shower?" his wife asked. "You've done that before."

Confusion crossed the author's face. "I don't think so. But I can go check."

"I saw it on your wrist before you got up to speak," Charlotte said.

A knot twisted in Faith's belly. *Is this another theft?* She spotted Kate supervising the clearing of the serving dishes at the buffet table and went over to her. "Can I have a word?" Faith asked.

Kate raised her brows. "Sure thing." To her helper, she said, "Be careful taking the cart through to the kitchen, okay?" She followed Faith to a corner.

"I think someone stole Oren's watch." Faith motioned to Charlotte and her friends, who were still searching. "He can't find it. He believes he left it on the podium, and now it's gone."

Kate tapped her lips with a finger. "There were tons of people in here, all milling around."

"Maybe one wanted a souvenir of their favorite author," Faith suggested. With Oren's fame and reputation, that had to be considered.

"Or the thief struck again." Kate narrowed her eyes. "Hold on. I'm going to get Marvin."

Faith joined the others at the head table. "Any luck?"

Charlotte shook her head, dropping the tablecloth edge she held. "We can't find it anywhere. It grew legs and walked off, I guess."

Oren's face had gone gray. "I wouldn't mind so much except it was a gift from my father upon the publication of my first book." He slumped down into a chair.

Lorraine knelt beside him. "We'll find it. Let's put up a notice. Perhaps someone will turn it in."

"That's the price of fame. A deranged fan probably stole it." Avis snorted. "I've had all kinds of things pilfered over the years. One nut even picked up my lip balm from a conference table."

Ugh. Faith exchanged a disgusted look with Taylor. "Kate—the server—went to get the manager," Faith said. "Maybe he can help."

A moment later Marvin bustled in. After greeting Oren and Lorraine effusively, he asked in a sprightly tone, "How can I be of assistance?"

Behind him, Kate rolled her eyes.

Oren didn't speak, so Lorraine said, "Oren's watch is missing. We think someone took it from the podium while he was signing books."

The manager drew himself up. "How can that be? Who would do such a thing here at the Lighthouse Bay Country Club?"

"Probably one of his fans," Avis said with a chuckle. "It happens to me all the time."

Marvin gave her the once-over. "I haven't had the pleasure." His voice rose in inquiry.

Avis appeared miffed. "I'm Avis Roth, *the* New York literary agent." The way she stressed *the*, one might have thought she was the only agent in the city.

"Of course." The manager turned back to Oren and Lorraine. "I'm certain the watch is merely misplaced. We can put up a sign at the front desk." He snapped his fingers at Kate. "Get a description from these folks and do that, okay?" With wishes for a good day, he left.

Kate sighed. "I guess I better get to work." Pulling out her notepad, she sat in the chair beside Oren. "What does your watch look like?"

As the author began to describe it in detail, Charlotte said to Faith, "Let's go. I need to get home for my rest time or Wolfe will scold me." She took Faith's arm. "Have you ever been scolded by Wolfe?" She smiled. "It's not fun."

I hope I never find out. With a final glance at Kate and Oren, Faith allowed Charlotte to steer her out of the room.

Tinkling piano notes drifted through the halls of Castleton, guiding Faith to the banquet hall. Dressed in a beaded gold gown, a glittering band across her forehead and a matching gold clutch in her hand, she felt as if she had stepped decades into the past.

As she strode through the Main Hall, her heels tapping on the marble, Wolfe emerged from the elevator, magnificent in white tie and tails.

Faith sucked in a breath. He might have walked off the pages of a Fitzgerald novel.

Noticing her, he stopped to wait. "You're lovely tonight. The 1920s look very good on you."

She laughed. "I'm glad you think so. It's rather enjoyable dressing up this way. I feel like I'm in a movie or something."

Wolfe held out his arm for her to take. "Or that we've slipped through a portal to an earlier time at Castleton." He paused in front of a portrait. "Witness my ancestors."

The portrait showed a woman in a dress similar to Faith's. A man stood behind her, his hand on the chair back.

Faith examined the painting, feeling a wistful tug of nostalgia. "It must be nice having such a wonderful record of your family's history." Her family had only a few heirlooms, and they were mostly tucked away in trunks and boxes.

"With such a legacy comes great responsibility," he said, his voice somber. He resumed walking, and they rounded a corner and entered the final stretch to the banquet hall.

Avis and Eban stood a short distance down the corridor.

Hildegarde, Lorraine, and Taylor looked on, and a few other guests milled around nearby.

Eban held his manila envelope out to the agent.

Avis put both hands up. "No way. I'm not taking that." She leaned forward, her face twisted in a snarl. "Get out of here, you talentless hack. You work in the garden, right? You should use that abomination you call a book as mulch."

Taylor winced, turning her head away.

"Chew it up and spit it out." Avis made grinding sounds.

Eban's face blanched. "But . . . Faith said it was good." Visibly shaking, he clutched the envelope to his chest.

"Faith?" Avis scoffed. "Who is Faith?" Her gaze fell on the person in question, and she had the grace to redden. She waved her hand at Eban. "Away with you. Go home, little boy."

Hunching his shoulders, Eban began to shuffle off. After a few steps, he stopped and whirled around. "You think you're so high-and-mighty. But one day you'll go too far. Someone is going to strike back."

One guest made a faint clapping sound.

Avis glared at the guest and shivered in mock fright. "I'm scared." She turned to her assistant. "Let's go. I'm starved, and if it's anything like lunch, the hordes will decimate the food before we get any."

"What a piece of work," Wolfe muttered. He reached out to Eban as he trudged by. "Don't let her get to you. Believe in yourself."

"Thanks, Mr. Jaxon. But it's not easy when an expert says you have no talent." He raised the envelope. "Maybe I should shred this baby."

"Don't you dare!" Righteous rage speared through Faith. "It's an excellent book. I'll help you find a publisher, okay?" She surprised herself with this rash promise, but she meant it.

Wolfe glanced at her with admiration. "I'll help too. If Faith says it's good, I believe her."

Tears shone in Eban's dark eyes. He blinked rapidly. "Thanks so much. It means more than I can say." He rushed away, probably embarrassed by his display of emotion.

Still arm in arm, Faith and Wolfe continued down the corridor. Faith tried to shake off the unpleasant scene and recapture the sense of magic she'd felt. Entering the banquet hall helped. Like many Castleton rooms, it had a soaring ceiling, this one adorned with sparkling circular chandeliers. The hearth had three openings, each filled with tall pillar candles instead of fires on this sultry night.

In the corner, Luis Gerardo, dressed to the nines like everyone else, sat at the baby grand, his nimble fingers coaxing out an upbeat tune. Something by Louis Armstrong, Faith guessed. Ivy, dressed in slinky satin, leaned against the piano, watching.

"There's Luis Gerardo," Wolfe said. "Shall I introduce you?"

"Please do." Faith's pulse quickened at the thrill of meeting a writer she admired.

Luis noticed their approach and wrapped up his song with a flourish. "Wolfe, my man." The writer slid off the bench, flapping his jacket tails into place, and held out a hand. "How are you?"

While Wolfe greeted him and made the introductions, Faith studied Luis closely. His dust jacket photo hinted at a smooth but warm charm. In person, that quality was readily apparent.

Ivy sashayed over to join them. She put a tiny hand on Wolfe's sleeve. "Remember me?" She batted her lashes. "I haven't been to Castleton in ages."

Wolfe rubbed his chin. "Hildegarde's granddaughter, right? I do remember you. Your mother brought you here right after you were born."

The reminder of her infant state seemed to take the wind out of the young woman's sails. "Yes, well, I guess it was a long time ago." She thrust her lower lip in a pout, then glanced at the tables where people were being seated. "I suppose we should claim a seat."

"It does look to be that time." Wolfe put his arm out for Faith. "Shall we?"

Brooke stopped them on the way to the table. "I found the perfect menu. It's from a dinner put on for President Coolidge."

Wolfe smiled. "I do admire your creativity. Thanks for getting into the spirit. Mother is so enjoying this."

Faith followed his gaze to the head table where Charlotte sat, lovely in a sequined dress and engaged in lively conversation.

Brooke couldn't repress a grin at her boss's praise. "Thanks, Mr. Jaxon." She noticed Marlene talking to the servers bringing in carts. "Oops, better run."

"Castleton is fortunate to have Brooke Milner," Wolfe said. "She really gave our menu a shot in the arm." He leaned closer. "It used to be so boring. Always chicken, rice, and carrots."

A typical conference meal.

This repast was much different, Faith discovered. The entrees included chicken à la rose, medallions of lamb, and aiguillette of striped bass. Seated beside Wolfe, Faith could only eat little bits of everything despite being famished from her meager lunch. Every time she got ready to take a mouthful, he would make a comment or ask her opinion.

After the main course ended, Faith excused herself to visit the ladies' room. Servers were clearing and bringing in the dessert carts, which looked amazing. Faith spotted strawberry shortcake, three-layer chocolate cake, lemon chiffon cake, and cream puffs.

The closest restroom was occupied, so Faith wandered down the hall to the next one. All the restrooms in the manor were large and luxurious, with stalls like small rooms. This one even had a separate powder room with sinks, a dressing table, and a fainting couch. Faith was about to leave when she heard the door open in the outer room.

"Good. No one is in here." Avis's voice.

Faith thought of calling out, but before she could, Taylor spoke. "What did you want to talk to me about?" Her voice held a note of anxiety.

Avis made a harrumphing sound. "It's not pretty when you learn your assistant, who should be loyal, is going behind your back."

"What do you mean? I'm not doing anything like that."

"You're seeing Luis, aren't you? And you know that I want him for my list." The way she said it reminded Faith of a hunter planning to bag big game.

"That's up to him, not me." Taylor sounded even more nervous. "He told me he's happy with his rep. He loves her."

"So. What. I can do more for him than that upstart. She only took him because she needed a client." Avis's voice dripped with disdain. "She lucked out."

Taylor muttered something.

"What was that? Speak up."

"I can't twist his arm. Besides, it's not, um, ethical to poach a client . . ." Her voice trailed away.

"I'll tell you what's not ethical. A deceitful assistant. If you don't shape up, I'll fire you. And I'll see to it that you'll never work in the industry again."

With that, one of them left, announced by the swish of the door.

Faith froze, sickened by the scene she had inadvertently witnessed. *Who was still in the room—Avis or Taylor?* A moment later, Faith heard sobbing. *Taylor.* To give her privacy, Faith waited. Finally she heard the door open again as Taylor left, a trio of laughing women entering as she did so.

Faith hurried out. She tried to convince herself it was none of her business. But somehow that assurance rang hollow.

Watson mewing in her ear prodded Faith awake the next morning too early for her liking. She'd been tossing and turning all night, worried about Taylor. The scene between Brooke's cousin and her boss had been disturbing to say the least. She wanted to confide in Brooke about it, but she hesitated to go behind Taylor's back, an argument she kept having with herself. She was exhausted.

After Watson resorted to taking a tentative nibble on her earlobe, she finally slid out of bed. "All right, Rumpy. Let's go have breakfast." She padded to the kitchen to put on coffee—after filling his dish, of course.

Cat and woman sat on the patio, listening to birdsong and enjoying the sun peeking through the trees.

Watson prowled the edge of the patio, sniffing the perimeter to make sure no intruders had breached his space. He was rustling around in a hydrangea bush when Faith heard a triumphant yowl.

A moment later, Watson reappeared, chasing Fitz the ferret. Fitz dashed behind the container of vegetables to hide, followed by Watson, who couldn't quite reach him.

"Not again." Faith's heart sank. All she needed to wreck her mood was another early-morning visit from the unpleasant agent.

The ferret chattered away in his hiding place, not sounding scared at all.

Watson gave up trying to push between the pots and lay down, purring. He'd made a new friend.

Avis didn't appear. With a sigh, Faith trudged into the house to call the manor. The lucky agent was probably sleeping in while her pet frolicked on the grounds.

The clerk picked up right away.

Faith recognized her voice. "Good morning, Cara. May I have Avis Roth's room, please?"

"Oh, she's not in. I saw her leave a while ago. She said she was taking a sunrise stroll." The clerk laughed. "She had that ferret with her. I've never seen one of those before. Cute little thing."

Faith thanked Cara and hung up. *That's odd. Avis and Fitz left the manor together. Where is Avis, then?*

Watson had abandoned his post guarding Fitz and was now winding his way around her ankles, meowing.

She looked down at the cat. "What is it?"

In answer he raced to the front door, still meowing.

This wasn't the first time Watson had tried to communicate something to her, so Faith slipped on sandals and followed.

He led her through the garden and to the main drive. Several times he ran ahead, pausing to glance over his shoulder to make sure she was still behind him.

Outside the gate, the narrow lane was lined with shady trees. Faith looked both ways, wondering which way Avis had gone. "Where is she, Watson?"

He veered left and trotted along the side, careful to stay out of the road proper. He had to be the smartest cat she knew.

Around the corner stood a huge maple on the left side of the road. Near the tree, Faith spotted an overturned pet carriage. It was bright green and hard to miss.

Beside the carriage lay a still human figure.

6

Faith's heart gave a single thud of shock, and then she burst into action. Watson at her side, she sprinted down the road and knelt beside the body, praying with all her might that Avis was alive. The agent lay facedown, unconscious.

Faith managed to find a faint pulse beating in the injured woman's wrist. Relief rushed through her, making her rock back on her heels. "She's alive, Watson! She's alive!"

He blinked at her, satisfied with the results of his efforts.

Faith reached into her pocket for her cell phone, only to realize she'd left it at home. She stood, clenching and unclenching her fists in anxiety, pondering the best course of action.

An automobile approaching from town made the decision for her.

Waving her arms and screaming like a demented person, she bolted down the road. Watson stayed with Avis.

The small sedan stopped, and the driver's side window rolled down. "What on earth is the matter?" Hildegarde asked.

"It's Avis. She's hurt." Faith pointed, her finger shaking. The adrenaline was ebbing away, and she was getting woozy. "Call 911."

"Avis is hurt? What happened?" Hildegarde fumbled around on the passenger seat, shoving aside her purse and a drugstore bag to locate her phone.

"I don't know. My cat found her. She's lying on the side of the road, unconscious."

Hildegarde dialed, then handed the phone to Faith. "Here you go. You can explain better than I can."

Keeping her teeth from chattering with a mighty effort, Faith described the situation to the dispatcher.

"Don't touch her," the official warned. "She may have a head or a spine injury. The medical technicians will be there in less than five minutes."

Faith gave the phone back to Hildegarde. "They're on their way."

"You stay with her. I'll go up to the manor and tell Charlotte and the others what happened," the older woman said.

"Tell Taylor. She needs to know." Faith jogged back to hold vigil over Avis with Watson. Hunkered down, Faith wished she could offer some comfort and aid, but she didn't dare touch Avis again after what the dispatcher had said.

Watson kept his distance too. He curled up under the big tree, his gaze never leaving Avis's face.

As promised, within minutes Faith heard the welcome shriek of sirens. The town ambulance flew up the road. Close behind was a police cruiser with Chief Garris at the wheel and Officer Bryan Laddy in the passenger seat.

The EMTs leaped out of their vehicle and went to work assisting Avis. "How long has she been lying here?" one asked Faith.

"I don't know, but the Castleton desk clerk might. She told me she saw Avis leave the manor."

"Looks like a hit-and-run accident," the other EMT said in a low voice.

Chief Garris addressed Faith. "Good morning. Why don't you take me through what happened?" He regarded her with kind, keen eyes that missed very little. Almost two decades older than Faith, the chief was always a reassuring and calming presence.

Feeling her shoulders slump in relief, she explained what she knew, beginning with the arrival of Fitz at her house.

Officer Laddy adjusted his glasses. "It's a good thing the little fellow came to see you," he remarked.

Faith gasped. "Oh no. Avis's ferret is still hiding on my patio." With the shock of discovering Avis, she had forgotten about the agent's pet.

"Don't worry. I'll send someone to retrieve him and make sure he's okay," the chief assured her.

The EMTs had Avis loaded on a gurney with an oxygen mask over her mouth and nose, and they gently slid her into the vehicle. "We're heading to the hospital, Chief," one called.

"We'll be along after we question a few people," Garris said. "Call me if her condition changes, will you?"

The EMT gave the chief a thumbs-up.

"Wait," Faith called. "Will she be okay?"

The EMT turned to her. "I sure hope so. We'll know more once she has a full examination." He jumped into the ambulance, and a moment later they roared off, sirens blaring.

"We'll go to the manor and ask if anyone saw anything." Garris pushed his hat back and scratched his head while he surveyed the landscape. "Not that it's likely since the house isn't visible from here." He settled his hat back in place.

"Surely if someone had seen her get hit they would have reported it," Faith said, appalled at the idea that a person wouldn't do something so simple to help someone else.

"They might not have seen the accident, but they may have seen the car." Garris gestured at the empty lane. "This isn't exactly the main drag."

"Here comes someone," Officer Laddy said, tipping his chin.

Faith and Chief Garris turned to see Eban pedaling a bicycle up the hill from town.

"He works here as a gardener," she told them.

Eban noticed them standing on the side of the road and instead of going up the driveway, he rode to where they stood. He braked beside the cruiser and hopped off the bike. "That was quick. I barely placed a call to the station."

Garris and Laddy exchanged glances.

"Are you speaking to us?" Garris asked.

"I sure am. Someone stole my car this morning. Or maybe it was last night. Either way, I got up to go to work and it was gone."

A missing car and a hit-and-run accident? Faith didn't believe in coincidences, but she managed to hold back the words rising in her throat. *Let the police do their job.*

Laddy had his notepad out. "What make and model?"

Eban shuffled his feet, seeming embarrassed to supply the details. "It's not worth much, but it's all I have, you know?" He gave them the description and the plate number.

"What color is it?" Laddy asked.

"It's blue. Mostly." Eban shrugged. "Accented with rust."

The officer stepped over to the cruiser and called the report in on the radio, mentioning the car may have been involved in a possible 480.

"What's that?" Eban asked Garris.

Garris set his lips in a thin line. "It's possible your car was involved in a hit-and-run accident this morning. Avis Roth was taken to the hospital a few minutes ago, hurt pretty badly." His gaze sharpened. "Is there anything you want to tell us?"

"An accident?" Eban wavered on his feet, almost losing his grip on the bicycle. "With my car?" The surprise on his face appeared genuine to Faith.

Garris stepped closer. "We don't know for sure until we find your car, but it's a bit odd that your car is missing and a woman was hit by one, don't you think?"

Eban had gone white under his tan. "Oh, man. I hope someone didn't run over that lady with my car."

The chief opened the rear door of the cruiser. "Have a seat. Tell me again when you noticed your car was missing."

The gardener propped his bicycle against a tree and obeyed, sitting sideways in the seat. "Like I said, when I got ready to come to work. I went out to the parking lot behind my building, and it was gone."

Faith decided it was time to make an exit. "Excuse me, Chief. I'll be at my cottage for a little longer and then over at Castleton if you need me. Please give me any updates regarding Avis."

"Will do, Faith. Thanks again." The chief turned back to Eban. Officer Laddy nodded to her.

With Watson at her heels, Faith trudged up the lane, sick at heart both for Avis and Eban. Two lives ruined in an instant, either by accident or deliberately.

Halfway up the drive, Taylor sprinted toward Faith from the other direction. She was dressed in running tights, a T-shirt, and sneakers. "I heard Avis is hurt. What happened?"

"They think she was hit by a car." Faith thought of something. "How did you find out?"

Taylor grabbed her arm. "Hildegarde told me you found Avis lying beside the road. Is she going to be all right?" The young woman's eyes widened as she waited for Faith's answer.

"I don't know. The ambulance crew wouldn't say." Faith slipped out of Taylor's grip. "I have to get ready for work. Walk with me if you want." She decided not to mention Eban being under suspicion, knowing that gossip had the power to ruin an innocent man's life. And so far there was no evidence that Eban's car had hit Avis, let alone that he had been at the wheel.

They walked in silence, interrupted only by occasional exclamations of shock and dismay from Taylor. Faith's thoughts were consumed by the memory of finding Avis, as well as the conversation she'd overheard the night before. Taylor's boss made her life miserable, but she seemed to be sincerely upset that Avis was hurt.

"Have you had breakfast?" Faith asked when they reached the cottage. "I haven't, and I really need to eat before going to work."

"I don't know if I can." Taylor grimaced, putting a hand to her midriff.

"At least have some toast. You need to keep up your strength." Realizing that she sounded like her grandmother, Faith didn't press the other woman further. In the kitchen, she ushered her to a seat, then put on fresh coffee and pulled eggs from the refrigerator. Scrambled eggs and toast would be light but filling.

At her feet, Watson crunched his second breakfast.

Someone knocked on the front door.

Faith went to answer it and found Brooke standing there. "Come in. Would you like some coffee?"

"An offer I can't refuse."

Faith led her friend to the kitchen, where Taylor sat huddled at the table.

"I didn't know you were here." Brooke bent over and gave her cousin a hug.

"I ran into Faith in the driveway." Taylor waved a hand. "I don't know what I was thinking. Avis had already gone to the hospital."

Brooke poured herself a cup of coffee. "Operating on instinct, rushing to see if you can help even if you know you can't." She leaned against the counter, watching while Faith cracked eggs into a blue bowl. "Got extra?"

Faith cracked another one. "I take it you're not on kitchen duty yet."

Brooke sipped the hot brew. "No, I'm serving lunch. I'm not officially due over there for an hour, so when I heard about Avis, I hurried over to see you." She watched Faith with concern. "Are you doing all right?"

Faith dumped the eggs into a pan. "Functioning." The tremors of an adrenaline aftermath were gone, but Faith knew from experience that the sense of nauseated disorientation would linger. She put four slices of bread in the toaster and pushed the levers down.

The sous-chef lowered her voice. "Eban is a suspect."

My, news does travel fast. Faith shot a glance at Taylor, who was studying the cup of coffee she held in both hands. "How did you hear that?"

"You know this town. Someone saw the police questioning him at the accident site. Then the dishwasher informed us that Eban's car was stolen." Brooke tapped her temple. "They're putting two and two together."

"I was afraid of that." Faith retrieved three plates from the cupboard and divided the eggs onto them. She added slices of buttered toast. "Can you find the jam in the fridge?"

Faith and Brooke joined Taylor at the table, and as the trio dug in, Taylor having found her appetite, someone knocked on the front door.

Both Brooke and Taylor froze, eyes wide.

Her heart in her throat, Faith walked to the door and opened it. She was alarmed to see Chief Garris. "Any news?" she managed to ask, dreading the answer.

A brief smile crossed his face. "I'm sorry. I didn't mean to frighten you. I'm looking for Taylor Milner. One of the gardeners said he noticed her walking with you earlier. Do you know where she is?"

"She's here. Come on in." Faith escorted him to the kitchen.

Taylor's fork clattered to her plate when she saw the chief. "Sorry," she muttered. "I'm so butterfingered today."

Brooke gave her a reassuring pat on the forearm.

The chief studied Brooke and Taylor. "I understand you two are cousins."

"We are," Brooke said. "We grew up in the same town too."

"Have a seat, Chief," Faith said. "Want coffee?"

"I wouldn't say no to a cup." Garris pulled out the chair across from Brooke and sat down, tucking his long legs under the table. He fixed his gaze on Taylor. "What's it like, working for a hotshot New York agent like Avis Roth?"

Faith knew the question was merely a gentle lead-in, as usual with Garris.

But Taylor cringed, hunching her shoulders. "It's okay. She can be tough." Then she bit her lip. She must have realized that she'd inadvertently opened the door to deeper probing.

The chief pulled out a notepad and a pen. "Tough, you say. How do you mean?" He smiled thanks when Faith set a mug in front of him.

Taylor's gaze skittered over the table, avoiding the chief. "Um, she's demanding. We're busy all the time, a lot of deadlines. You know, like that."

Brooke frowned at her cousin, her brows knitting together. She opened her mouth to say something, then apparently thought better of it.

Faith filled Brooke's cup and her own and sat at the table.

Garris let that line of questioning go for the moment. "When did you last see Ms. Roth?"

Taylor ran a hand through her hair. "Last night? After dinner, we went up to our rooms. I went to bed early because I was so wiped."

And so upset at being threatened with firing. If it had been Faith in Taylor's shoes, she would have been awake all night with stress.

"You didn't see her this morning?"

Taylor shook her head.

Garris asked, "What time did you get up?"

"Around six. I went out for a run." Taylor tugged at her tights. "I was on my way back to my room when Hildegarde Maxwell, one of the guests, told me Avis had been hurt. I went to see what was going on and ran into Faith. And that's it."

Garris diligently wrote all this down. "Is Ms. Roth a runner too?"

Taylor burst out laughing. She put a hand to her mouth. "Sorry. It's just that Avis is so not a runner. If it wasn't for Fitz, she wouldn't even go for walks."

The chief's brow wrinkled in confusion.

Faith jumped in. "Fitz is the ferret who came to see me and Watson. It was his bright green carriage on the road."

"Seriously, she walks him in a carriage?" Brooke's eyes danced with amusement. "I've seen dogs in those things, which is ridiculous enough. But a ferret?"

"Well, a ferret's legs are pretty short," Taylor reasoned. "Much shorter than even the tiniest dog."

Garris cleared his throat, a warning they had drifted off topic. "How often does Ms. Roth go out for these walks? Is it a regular thing?"

Taylor nodded. "She goes out every morning. And again at night."

"Someone knew she'd be on the road," Brooke blurted out. She put a hand to her mouth. "I shouldn't speculate."

Garris pushed back from the table and stood. "I'll be in touch. How long are you staying here, Miss Milner?"

Taylor tipped her head back to look up at him. "All week." A spasm of fear crossed her face. "Do you really think someone deliberately ran Avis over?"

The chief tucked away his notebook. "Too early to say. Don't leave town until this is sorted out, okay?" He turned to Faith. "I'll let myself out."

After he left, they sat in silence for a long moment.

"Wow," Taylor said. "I've never been interrogated by the police before. I felt like he thought I did it."

"Chief Garris is extremely fair," Faith said, rising to the officer's defense. "I think it's the nature of the job. He has to keep an open mind until all the facts are in."

"As long as you're telling the truth," Brooke said, "you have nothing to be afraid of."

Taylor looked down at her fingernails, her cheeks reddening.

What is she hiding? The assistant hadn't volunteered that she and her boss were on the outs, and Faith couldn't blame her. But she had an inkling there was more to it than the argument she overheard.

Brooke drained her cup and leaped up from her seat. "I hate to break up the party, but I'd better head to the manor. See you over there." She moved toward the door at her usual fast pace, then halted. "Wasn't Avis supposed to give a talk at lunch? I saw it on the schedule."

Faith groaned. "You're right. I forgot all about it. I wonder what we'll do on such short notice."

"Are you sure you're all right with this?" Charlotte asked. "We can skip the whole thing."

Charlotte, Faith, and Marlene were conferring before an outdoor lunch at the manor.

I'm not certain at all, but I really have no choice. That thought was reinforced when Faith met the assistant manager's steely gaze. "The show must go on, as they say," Faith said with a laugh. "It's bad enough Avis's condition is still uncertain without disappointing our guests."

"That's the spirit," Marlene said briskly. "You'll do fine." With that reassurance, she bustled away to check on the grills at the other end of the terrace. Huge vats of steamer clams and lobsters were on the fire, along with potatoes and corn on the cob.

At least lunch will be a hit. The smell of well-seasoned seafood drifted to her nose, making her mouth water.

Faith shuffled through her notes. To replace Avis's talk, she and Charlotte had decided on the topic of female writers in the 1920s. Faith had chosen to read excerpts from *Gentlemen Prefer Blondes*, the satirical 1925 novel by Anita Loos, and poems by Dorothy Parker.

When Charlotte rang a bell, the attendees chose seats at several long tables shaded with umbrellas. Faith sat at the end nearest the podium, where she would speak during dessert.

Brooke and her crew served the meal, the first course steamers with clam broth and butter. After the mounds of shells were cleared away, bright red lobsters and grilled vegetables were brought around. Faith forced her upcoming ordeal out of her mind and concentrated on dipping chunks of succulent lobster into butter.

"I've had lobster a million times, but it's still a treat." Hildegarde, seated to Faith's left, dipped a whole claw in her butter bowl. "Especially now that I've lost my husband, Francis."

Faith found the comment odd, but before she could ask Hildegarde what she meant, Brooke appeared at her shoulder.

"I've got news from Taylor," Brooke whispered. "Avis is going to be okay. She'll be discharged this evening." Then her face fell. "And I heard they found Eban's car. They think it's the one that hit her. Deliberately."

Faith was still unsettled by Brooke's news—both good and bad—when she launched into her presentation. She began automatically with an excerpt from the delightful Anita Loos satire, accompanied by remarks about the novel's best-selling status.

The audience, resembling a sea of hats thanks to their period garb, thankfully didn't seem to notice that she was distracted.

The memory of Avis's brutal treatment of the young writer sat in her chest like a stone. *Had anger and humiliation driven Eban to plan homicide? Or was the act impulsive, spurred by seeing the agent walking along the road? Or was his car actually stolen?*

After concluding the Loos portion, Faith moved on to Dorothy Parker, famed writer and wit. Parker had been an integral part of the Algonquin Round Table, a group of New York writers, editors, and actors.

"This next poem is very familiar to most of you, I imagine," Faith said. "Called 'Résumé,' it's a tongue-in-cheek summary of suicide methods and their drawbacks."

The crowd snickered.

As Faith read, she pictured Eban behind the wheel, rage flashing over him, followed by a terrible split-second decision. But what about Fitz? Had he noticed Avis pushing Fitz along? Surely that bright green carriage was impossible to miss.

No, she couldn't imagine Eban hurting the innocent animal, no matter how disagreeable his owner might be.

Movement at the back of the terrace created a disruption, and the audience turned to watch Luis and Ivy saunter in. They settled in chairs at the edge of the crowd.

Faith took a moment to regroup before reading the next poem. Once again she knew it so well she didn't have to concentrate. Instead, her attention was captured by Ivy whispering to Luis and showing him something on her phone.

A lady seated nearby shushed them loudly.

Ivy slipped out a few minutes later and headed around the side of the house.

Almost immediately, Taylor emerged through the terrace door and scanned the throng. Luis waved and she hurried to join him, perching on Ivy's vacated chair.

Brooke, watching from near the buffet table, arched her brows at this game of musical chairs.

Faith sighed. *Almost done.* "To conclude, ladies and gentlemen, I'm going to read 'Love Song.'" The poem started like a romantic poem and ended with a funny, unexpected line, a perfect punctuation point.

The group responded as she hoped, bursting into laughter and applause.

"Thank you, Faith. That was lovely," Charlotte said. "This afternoon and evening are free time. We encourage you to avail yourselves of Castleton's wonderful facilities, including a spa, a pool, a beach, these wonderful gardens, and, of course, our excellent library. But don't forget, tomorrow at dinner there will be an author talk with Oren Edwards and Luis Gerardo, two American greats."

The onlookers clapped again, many beaming at Luis. As they dispersed, a few greeted him.

After all the guests left, Charlotte came up to Faith. "Did you hear the news about Avis? She's going to be all right, thank goodness."

"Yes, Brooke told me right before I went on. I'm so relieved," she said, tucking her notes into her tote.

Charlotte stepped closer, lowering her voice although no one was within earshot. "I heard that they think Eban did it." She frowned. "I've asked Marlene to put him on leave while they investigate. I hated to do that, but I'm afraid having him here will create problems."

Poor Eban. Hot indignation rose in Faith's chest. "He reported his car stolen. I was there when he talked to the police. Maybe he's innocent."

Charlotte sighed, staring across the grounds. "I hope so. I hate to think one of our trusted employees would do such a thing."

Faith held back further objections but added, "If he's cleared, does he get his job back?"

"Of course. I'm trying to protect him as well as Castleton right now." A smile played across Charlotte's lips, and her eyes were lit with amusement. "You're quite the champion of the underdog, aren't you?" She spotted Watson, who had decided to join them on the terrace after napping for a couple of hours in the library. "Or should I say under-cat?"

Faith laughed. "Cats always come out on top. That's what Watson would say."

"I'm sorry, but I refuse to believe Eban is guilty." Kate crossed her arms over her chest.

Next to her, around the Fosters' patio table, Midge, Brooke, Faith, and Eileen sipped glasses of iced coffee adorned with fresh mint from the garden. Kate had the night off from the country club so she had joined them for an impromptu dinner.

"I don't blame you, sugar," Midge drawled. Raised in the South, Midge retained a touch of a charming Southern accent. "You've been close friends with him since grade school."

"I know him too," Eileen said. "He's a fine young man, a regular at the Candle House Library since kindergarten."

"That's how Eileen judges people," Midge teased. "By their library memberships or lack thereof." She turned toward her husband, Peter, who was manning the grill. "You remember Eban Matthews, don't you, honey?"

Peter stabbed a chicken breast with a fork and set it on a platter. "Of course I do. He was always regaling me with his mountain-climbing adventures." He grimaced. "I recall one of them ended in disaster, though. I think one of the climbers died."

"He wrote a fantastic book based on that tragedy," Faith said. "But instead of taking him on as a client, Avis rejected him brutally, right in public." She shuddered. "I felt terrible for him. It was humiliating."

"Are they using that as a motive?" Midge asked.

"I guess so," Faith said. "What else is there, as far as Eban is concerned?"

Brooke tipped her head, looking thoughtful. "If he's innocent, then who did it?"

Kate's cheeks were still flushed with anger. "Good question. She's not the nicest lady. I know that much from seeing her at the club."

Peter set the platter of chicken on the table. "Dig in." He sat beside his wife and reached for the salad bowl, which he held out to Faith, seated on his other side. "This is all from our garden."

"It's beautiful." Faith admired the colorful array of fresh vegetables in the bowl as she served herself a healthy amount.

"All the credit belongs to Peter," Midge said. "He's the one with the green thumb in this family."

Faith passed the salad to Brooke. Next potato salad and chicken came around. Faith filled her plate with a laugh. "I can't believe I'm eating this much after having lobster for lunch at Castleton."

Peter whistled. "Lobster for lunch? Mrs. Jaxon is really going all out for this affair, isn't she?"

"She certainly is," Faith agreed. "There's a wonderful lineup of events. We have a 1920s fashion show, an antique car race, and a Gatsby Ball coming up." Her stomach lurched when she remembered Wolfe's offhand remark about saving a dance for him. *Did he mean it? Or was he only joking?*

"It all sounds great. You're going to have a fabulous time," Eileen said.

"You'll have to learn the Charleston." Humming, Midge swayed her arms back and forth, almost elbowing her daughter.

"Mother!" Kate ducked aside with a scowl. "How can you talk about a dance when my friend's future is in jeopardy?"

Midge sobered. "I'm sorry, dear. You're right. We need to find out who did that terrible thing." She snapped her fingers and swayed again. "Then we can do the Charleston in celebration."

Kate rolled her eyes.

"Is there anyone else at Castleton with a strong motive?" Eileen asked. "Maybe one of them stole Eban's car to divert suspicion to him."

"Oren Edwards isn't very happy with Avis. She's his agent." Faith told them about Oren's disagreement with Avis and what his wife had said about her opinion of his new book. "If your agent dumps you, that would probably have a huge effect on your career, right?"

Peter settled his glasses on his nose. "If your career is on the decline, I'd think it might. It would be perceived as a vote of no confidence."

"For a man whose reputation is wrapped up in his books, that would be quite a blow," Eileen noted.

Brooke was jotting down notes on a paper napkin. "So Oren has a motive. Who else?"

Faith thought of Luis and Ivy. "This probably isn't related in the least, but Luis Gerardo and Ivy Maxwell spend a lot of time together. But Avis said Taylor is dating him."

"Even though we're cousins," Brooke said, "I hate to pry into Taylor's personal affairs."

"See, Mom?" Kate's tone was triumphant. "Some people keep their noses out of their relatives' business."

"You're not just my relative. You're my daughter," Midge said. To the others, she commented, "She's still mad we nixed her prom date."

"He was so cute," Kate moaned. But the twinkle in her eyes revealed she was teasing her parents.

Faith steered the conversation back to Luis. "I know Avis rejected Luis in the past, but he's famous now. So why would he hold a grudge?"

"He wouldn't," Eileen said. "He should be sending her flowers in thanks for the rejection. Obviously he has the right agent for his work. Perhaps she wasn't it."

"I'll write his name down anyway," Brooke said. "And Ivy's too. Maybe once we start digging we'll learn something."

"Another person in the inner circle is Hildegarde Maxwell. Her husband, Francis, was a famous editor." Faith remembered something. "Hildegarde was out doing an errand when Avis was hit." She told them how Hildegarde had come along and called 911 for Faith.

"Do you think she was really doing an errand?" Brooke asked. "Maybe she hit Avis and went around the block." She pursed her lips. "Long block, though. That road goes way out along the coast."

"I think she was." Faith shrugged. "I saw a bag from the downtown drugstore on the front seat of her car."

"Early-morning drugstore run?" Eileen shook her head. "Poor woman." Faith's aunt suffered from rheumatoid arthritis, although she downplayed her symptoms and the limitations and discomfort of the ailment.

The table was silent for a moment, and then Faith asked Kate, "Anything new regarding the missing items at the country club?"

"Did you find your earrings?" Brooke chimed in.

Kate sighed and glanced at her mother. "Not yet. At least nothing else has gone missing since Oren Edwards's watch disappeared."

"What's this?" Eileen asked. "Someone stole his watch?"

"I forgot you weren't there," Faith said. Eileen had been unable to attend the luncheon due to appointments. "We think Oren left his watch on the podium and someone took it while he was signing books."

"It must have been a fan," Kate said. "That's what the manager insisted, anyway. The problem is people misplace things all the time at the club. It's hard to know what is lost and what's been stolen."

"Except your earrings," Peter said with calm certainty. "You put them in your purse, and now they're gone."

Kate blinked back tears. "I haven't given up on finding out who did it." She toyed with the napkin in her lap. "Even though the police basically said it would be a long shot to locate them."

"I'm glad you filed a report." Faith had an idea. "Why don't you draw us a picture so we can keep our eyes open for them?"

"Many thieves aren't very smart," Eileen said with a chuckle. "At least we have that advantage."

Brooke sat up straight, smoothing her short hair into place with both hands. "That's true. We're bright *and* in the right."

The others laughed.

"On that note," Midge said, standing, "who wants dessert?"

Someone's phone jingled.

"That's mine." Kate searched around for her phone, finding it on a nearby lounge chair. "It's Eban. What if he's been arrested?"

The group froze in silent anticipation when Kate answered the call. Midge even paused on her way to the sliding glass door. Faith sat tense, fists clenched, while she waited to learn the news.

"Hey, Eban. What's up?" Kate bit her lip, frowning in concentration. Then her face cleared, an easing of tension. "Hang in there, okay? See you tomorrow at the club."

"What did he say?" Midge asked before Kate fully disconnected.

Kate set her phone on the table. "You won't believe this. An eyewitness came forward and said they saw Eban's car on the road this morning." She smiled. "With a woman at the wheel."

Brooke gave a whoop. "A woman? Then it definitely wasn't Eban." She comically wiggled her brows up and down.

"So it looks like your friend is off the hook," Peter said.

"Almost," Kate replied. "They told him not to leave town. I guess they want to make sure he wasn't in on it with someone."

Eileen snorted. "Remember what I said about the criminal mind? I doubt even a criminal would use his own vehicle for a hit-and-run accident."

"Good point," Faith said. Her mind began to churn with theories.

Midge pulled on the slider handle. "I think we need my strawberry shortcake to celebrate."

Everyone at the table groaned.

"You know y'all want some." Flashing a wicked smile, Midge vanished into the house.

The cat crept along the corridor, ducking behind a huge urn when a human pushing a trolley full of dishes rattled past. The human pressed the button on the box, and when the doors opened, he shoved the cart inside.

The cat hated that box. It moved so fast it felt like it was pulling off his fur.

He reached the staircase, challenging himself to see how fast he could race up the steps. The apartment door was open, as it often was during the days when the nice lady was in residence. Tonight he was here to check on his furry friend.

Inside the apartment, the cat followed the scent trail, entering a vast room holding sofas and chairs in groupings. The light was low, with only a couple of lamps lit. He was halfway across the carpet when a man and a woman entered the room, forcing him to dash for cover.

They settled on the sofa right over his head. He was trapped. With a sigh, he lay down, resting his head on his paws.

"I can't believe the old witch survived that accident," the man said. "What does she have, nine lives?"

The cat's ears perked up. Nine lives was the prerogative of cats.

"Shh." A giggle. "Be nice."

"So she lives another day to torture us poor writers." The sound of hands rubbing together and a cackle. "'Whose dreams can I demolish today?'"

"Stop it. Being bitter doesn't become you."

A yawn. "You know what I could use? A slice of that chocolate cake." The sound of springs squeaking. "Coming?"

"All right. But I'm not eating any cake."

Laughter. "That's what you always say."

Their footsteps thudded away.

The cat streaked across the room to the bedroom where the ferret lived. The door here was also slightly ajar. He nudged it open with his paw and slipped inside.

The nice lady was standing by the bed, bending over the mean one.

"You really should get some rest. Let me take your phone and put it away so people don't bother you."

The mean one held the object close to her chest. "No way. I need to make some calls first thing in the morning. This phone is my lifeline."

The cat skulked along the wall, careful to stay out of view. He paused behind a standing mirror to sniff for his friend.

"I'll refill this pitcher of water." The nice lady lifted the container off the nightstand. "And if you want something else to eat, I'll be glad to get it for you."

"I'm fine. Thank you." She watched as her friend walked across the carpet toward the bathroom. "You know what that accident taught me?"

The nice lady paused. "To enjoy life more fully?"

"Ha ha. No. To take care of business while I still can." She clutched the phone closer. "Heads will roll."

The other woman shook her head. "You're something else."

After she passed in front of the cat's hiding place, he darted to the cage holding the ferret, tucked next to the bureau.

Happy to see him, his friend chattered and chirped.

The cat lay on the carpet and purred.

The next morning, Faith decided to detour to the seaside lavender garden, one of her favorite spots at Castleton. With all that was on her mind, she could use a few minutes gazing at the ocean while inhaling calming fragrances. The pocket garden featured white and pink lavender among the more classic purples.

Watson came along, stopping now and then to investigate interesting aromas and sights along the path.

As she drew closer to the water, the gentle sound of waves breaking on the beach drifted to her ears. Seagulls wheeled overhead, crying and squawking. She paused to take a deep breath, relishing the distinctive salty odor of the sea. What a pleasure it was to live within sight and sound of the ocean.

The garden was accessed through a break in a cedar hedge. Faith stepped through, only to be confronted by the sight of Taylor and Lorraine sitting together on a bench. She must have startled them, because they both jumped.

An oddly furtive expression crossed Taylor's face. "Hi, Faith," she said. "Fancy meeting you here."

"Sorry to intrude," Faith said, backing up. She bumped into something soft. Whirling around, she saw Avis Roth standing right behind her, a ferocious glare on her face. She had one foot wrapped in a bandage and was leaning on a crutch. Faith wondered how the woman had made it down here from the manor.

"Leaving so soon?" Avis's grin resembled that of a shark. She lifted the crutch, gesturing with it. "Step into the garden, my dear."

"Oh no, I really should get going." Despite her protest, Faith found herself pushed through the hedge by Avis's bullish advance. The flailing crutch dispersed any lingering resistance.

As for Watson, he ducked under the foliage and went inside that way, well out of Avis's reach.

Once Avis and Faith were inside the garden proper, the agent fixed the other two women with a cold stare. "What's going on here?"

"Nothing. We're just chatting." Taylor's cheeks flushed, giving the lie to her words. She folded her hands and looked down at them.

"That's right, Avis." Lorraine sucked in air with an exaggerated breath. "We're enjoying the calming lavender scent. You ought to try it."

Avis continued to glare beneath lowered brows. "Are you implying I need to calm down?" Her voice was deadly, the words spit through clenched teeth. "On the contrary, I do my best work when I'm riled up."

Lorraine rose from the bench. "Should you even be out here in the garden? Surely you need to rest."

"I'm fine." Avis waved her crutch. "A little banged up and bruised but I'll live."

Faith sidled toward the exit. "Charlotte must be looking for me—"

Avis gripped Faith's arm. "You're not going anywhere, missy." She paused for a long, charged moment, then blurted out, her words like bullets, "You're fired, Taylor. How dare you try to poach a client?"

Taylor shrank back against the bench, the color draining out of her face. She began to cry, putting both hands over her eyes to hide the tears.

Lorraine wasn't cowed. "I'm not your client, Avis. And after the way you've treated my husband, I never will be. Taylor loves my romance novel, and she'll find it a good home."

Avis sneered. "No, she won't. She's not an agent. After I get done with her, no reputable agency will hire her."

Lorraine gasped. "Why are you so vindictive?" A look of pity crossed her features. "What on earth do you get out of it?"

The agent whirled around, pushing Faith aside with a sweep of her arm. "Plenty. How do you think I've made it this far? By being nice?" She lurched away, stabbing the crutch into the soft turf.

Faith lingered, not sure what to do, wanting to escape but feeling heartless if she left Taylor wailing in anguish.

Lorraine slid across the bench and put her arm around the young woman. "Hush, darling. We'll find you a new job. Oren will help."

Watson leaped up beside Taylor, cuddling close to her from the other side.

Taylor scrubbed at her face with the back of one hand. "But you heard what she said. She's going to have me blacklisted. No one will take me on. Ever." With a tiny smile, she reached out and rubbed Watson's chin.

"Let me know if I can do anything to help." Faith glanced at her phone. She had been due at Charlotte's five minutes ago. "I hate to run off, but I need to go to work."

The other two glanced up at Faith as though they'd forgotten she was there.

"Faith, can you please tell Brooke what happened?" Taylor sniffed, fighting back a fresh bout of tears. "I suppose I'll have to move out of Castleton. The agency paid for my room."

Lorraine patted her on the back like a mother comforting a child. "You shouldn't stay here anyway. Why see Avis more than you have to? Go to your cousin's. You can still come to the conference events. As my guest."

"I'll detour by the kitchen and talk to Brooke," Faith told Taylor. The detour would make her even later, but it couldn't be helped.

"Would you?" Taylor's eyes were plaintive. "I'll feel better once I know I have somewhere to land."

"Let's go to the manor and order some reviving tea," Lorraine suggested. She helped Taylor to her feet. "We'll sit on the terrace."

Without waiting for them to follow, Faith jogged through the hedge, Watson racing along beside her. She chose a shortcut that skirted the maze and led through the rose garden, a confection of pink and red and white blossoms filled with buzzing bees. After crossing a quiet expanse of lawn and taking a brief tour of the kitchen garden, she was at the lower level entrance.

Her hand was on the handle of the screen door when someone opened it from the other side.

"Good morning." Eban pointed at his Castleton polo with a big grin. "Look who's been reinstated." He jabbed a thumb toward the upper stories. "I have Charlotte to thank. According to Marlene, she insisted that I come back."

"I'm so happy for you." Faith glanced around to make sure no one was in earshot. "Do you have any idea who took your car?"

Eban ran a hand through his hair, his brow furrowed. "I honestly don't. I park at the edge of the grocery store parking lot since the lot at my apartment building is always full."

"You didn't see who took it?" Faith asked him again, even though he'd already denied it.

"Nope. I couldn't even if I tried. There's a tall line of cedar trees between my building and the parking lot."

Faith pictured the layout. Next time she went to the grocery store, she'd have to look more closely at the parking lot. Not that it would do much good at this late date.

Eban glanced toward the path leading to the garages. "Nice talking to you, but I'd better get going. There's a lot of lawn to mow." He grinned again. "I don't want to get fired for being late."

"Me neither. See you later." With a wave, Faith went into the building. The lower level housed the kitchen, laundry, and various offices. Telling Watson to stay put in the hall, she peeked around the kitchen door, not wanting to get in the way. The room was a hive of activity, with cooks chopping, sautéing, and stirring in a hubbub that was deceptively chaotic.

Brooke was at the stove tasting a sauce. She nodded in approval. "That's excellent. Just add a tiny bit more pepper and salt."

A young woman dicing vegetables noticed Faith. "Brooke, you've got company."

Wiping her hands on her apron, Brooke sidled out from behind the counter to join Faith. "Want a cup of coffee?" Smiling, she picked up a plate filled with baked goods and displayed it to her friend. "I've got cinnamon buns." Her voice was a teasing singsong.

"I wish I could, but I need to get upstairs." Faith glanced around at the busy kitchen. "Do you have a minute? I have something to tell you."

Brooke set the plate down, her smile fading. "It sounds serious."

They stepped into the hallway, and Faith quickly filled her in on the scene she'd reluctantly witnessed. "I told Taylor I'd let you know what happened."

Brooke shook her head. "Avis actually fired her in front of witnesses? That's awful. But it sounds like Taylor's better off not working for her, even if she is a top agent."

"From what I've seen, I'd say that's true."

"I need to finish up a couple things in here," Brooke said, "and then I'll go find her. Did she say where she'd be?"

"Having tea on the terrace with Lorraine Edwards." Faith checked the clock on the wall. "Now I'd better fly. Charlotte is waiting for me."

In the interest of saving time, Faith and Watson took the elevator to the apartment on the third floor, despite Watson's reluctance. Upstairs Faith and Watson made their way to the office, the designated meeting place.

The office door was slightly ajar, and with a knock, Faith pushed it open. Papers were scattered across the table and the curtains were open to the sunlit view, but there was no sign of Charlotte.

"Maybe she's in the kitchen," Faith said to Watson. She had started to back out of the room when she heard a groan. "Mrs. Jaxon?" she called.

In answer, she heard another groan. It seemed to come from a group of sofas at the far end of the room.

Heart in her throat, Faith trod across the carpet to see who or what was making that terrible sound.

Charlotte lay on one of the couches, her arm across her eyes.

9

"Mrs. Jaxon, are you all right?" Faith knelt beside the sofa, uncertain about what to do. Wolfe's concerns ran through her head. Should she call him?

As if sensing that Charlotte was unwell, Watson kept his distance instead of jumping up as he normally would have.

Charlotte opened one eye. "I felt dizzy so I lay down for a minute." She promptly shut that eye again. "Oh, I'm still woozy." She flapped a hand toward a blood pressure cuff lying on the floor. "The reading was really low."

Faith didn't hesitate now. She dialed Wolfe, hoping that he was available. Blood pressure that was too low could lead to shock and even death.

Thankfully he picked right up. "Faith, how are you?"

"I'm fine," she said, "but I'm concerned about your mother. She says her blood pressure is too low."

"I'll be right there. I'm out in the gardens talking to the head groundskeeper. Give her a big glass of water, okay?"

Faith raced to obey, grateful a pitcher of water and glasses had been set on the credenza for their use during the meeting. She ferried the full glass to Charlotte. "Can you sit up? Wolfe said to drink this. He's on his way."

The older woman scooted to an upright position and took the glass. She drank every drop, wiped her mouth in an unusually inelegant gesture, and handed the glass back to Faith. "Thank you, dear."

Thundering footsteps were heard, and Wolfe burst into the room. He waved his phone. "The doctor is on her way."

Faith moved aside so he could kneel beside Charlotte. He took her wrist and felt for her pulse.

"Don't fuss, Wolfe." Charlotte yanked her hand away. "I'll be all right. In fact, I'm already feeling better. I think the medication made my blood pressure drop too much."

"That's not good. We need to get that figured out." Wolfe rose, then picked up the blood pressure cuff. "And you're resting today."

"I can't rest," Charlotte protested. "We need to finish planning tomorrow's fashion show, and tonight is the presentation by Oren and Luis. We've got a full house staying here for both—and many outside guests coming."

His answer was a grunt. "Let's take a reading." He slid the cuff over his mother's slender arm and secured it in place. "Faith, please go wait for the doctor by the apartment door." He noticed the cat. "You can stay or go, Watson, as you choose."

With a mew, he leaped up onto the window seat and began to wash.

"There's his answer," Charlotte said with a laugh.

The doctor soon arrived, and Faith led her to the office, then excused herself to give them privacy. Out in the living room, she consulted her binder. Fashion show model selection was scheduled for one that afternoon in the Great Hall Gallery. The evening presentation was all set, with the authors both speaking about how F. Scott Fitzgerald had influenced them and what it meant to be considered a voice of a generation.

After about fifteen minutes, Wolfe appeared in the office door. "You can come in now, Faith."

"The crisis appears to be over." The doctor was packing up her instruments. "I'll call in the adjusted prescription right now. But it wouldn't hurt for you to take it easy for a day, Charlotte."

"I suppose," Charlotte said, then brightened. "How about I let Faith take the lead, and I'll be a spectator?"

Everyone turned to Faith.

Nothing like being put on the spot. "Today's agenda is fairly light. We're choosing models for the fashion show at one, and then there's nothing until dinner. And I'm sure the kitchen staff has that under control."

Charlotte clasped her hands together. "I do want to help pick the models. I need to make sure they suit the vintage clothing I've had brought in."

"What's this fashion show?" the doctor asked. "It sounds interesting."

"We're doing a Great Gatsby fashion show," Charlotte said. "With both men's and women's fashions. It's going to be spectacular." She gestured at Faith's frock, a delicate eyelet drop-waist dress trimmed with pink. "In the spirit of this week, I've had many of the staff wear 1920s garb."

The doctor smiled at Faith. "I was wondering about that. I thought perhaps you had a fondness for styles from the past."

Again feeling put on the spot, Faith said, "I do. They're actually very comfortable."

"And becoming." Wolfe's gaze met hers, and she blushed.

The doctor took her leave, and Charlotte and Faith sat at the table, Charlotte staying in the office despite Wolfe's continued objections.

"If you feel the least bit dizzy again, I insist you tell Faith," Wolfe said. "And, Faith, you make her rest. If she refuses, call me, okay?"

Charlotte smiled at her son. "You are a bossy one, aren't you? All right, I promise."

"I'll see you two later. I'm working from home today." Halfway to the door, he halted. "By the way, do either of you know what happened with Taylor Milner? I saw her carting a suitcase out of the apartment."

Faith sucked in a breath, darting a glance at Charlotte. *Will this upset her?*

"Go ahead," Charlotte said. "I'm a big girl."

"Avis fired Taylor this morning. I think Taylor was on her way to Brooke's apartment, where she'll be staying."

Wolfe sighed, and Faith could tell by the look on his face that he wanted to say something. But he bit his lip. Finally he said, "Well, it's none of our business. See you at lunch."

"Let's have it on the terrace," Charlotte called. "Have a good morning."

A staff member knocked and came into the room. "I have the mail." He set a basket brimming with letters, flyers, and manila envelopes on the table.

Charlotte thanked him by name, one of her gracious touches, and sorted through the heap. Wolfe's pile was quite large. Charlotte picked up a plain envelope and frowned. "What is this?" She showed it to Faith.

The envelope had no stamp or return address, and Avis's name was written across it in a scrawl. "Maybe a personal note?"

"But it was in with the regular mail." Charlotte thrust the envelope out to Faith. "Can you please give this to Avis? It might be important."

"Of course." Inwardly Faith quailed, wanting to minimize any contact with the hateful agent. She took a deep breath and went in search of Avis.

She found Avis in the dining room, seated at the head of the table with folders and papers strewn in front of her. Muttering to herself, she was reading through a thick manuscript and making notes with a red pen.

Faith cleared her throat when Avis didn't seem to notice her.

The woman glared over her reading glasses. "What is it?"

"I have a letter for you." Faith approached the table, the envelope extended.

Avis snatched it and ripped it open, then scanned the page inside. She dropped it, then sank back in her seat, hand over her heart, as deflated as a limp balloon. "Another threat," she croaked.

"May I?"

Avis gestured to the page. "Be my guest."

Faith scooped up the paper, careful to hold it by the edges. Typed, it was short and to the point.

You were lucky this time.

Fear twisted in Faith's midsection. "We need to call the police."

"What good will that do? They didn't save me from getting run over." Avis leaned her head back and closed her eyes. "Oh, go ahead and call them."

Faith placed the call and reached Chief Garris.

"I'll be right over," he said. "By the way, can you find out if Eban Matthews is on-site? I need to ask him a few more questions."

Did Eban send the note? "He's here, Chief. I saw him about an hour ago."

"Good. See you in a few." He disconnected.

"The chief will be over soon." Faith studied the agent, who appeared ill. Her face was pale and her forehead sweaty. "Will you be all right if I leave you for a minute? I need to tell Charlotte what's going on." *Without triggering a stress attack.*

Predictably, Avis glowered. "I'll be fine. Pour me a glass of water, will you?"

Faith complied, then made her way back across the huge apartment to the office.

"I was beginning to wonder where you were," Charlotte said. "I've put the outfits in categories so we can figure out how many models we need. I'm thinking six of each gender." She showed Faith the list. "They'll come out in scenarios. Casual, evening, sporting—"

"Hold on a second. I—well, I'll just spit it out. Avis got another threat, and the chief is on his way over." Faith held her breath, watching Charlotte closely.

Charlotte burst into laughter. "You should see your face. Don't worry. I'm not planning to drop dead on you." She pushed back from the table. "Let's go support Avis."

Watson yawned and stretched on the window seat.

"You too, Rumpy," Charlotte said. At Faith's—and Watson's— surprised expressions, she added, "I've heard you call him that. It's so cute."

Watson's scowl said otherwise.

Chief Garris took the note seriously and placed it in a clear, labeled bag as evidence. "Who handled this? We'll need to take prints for elimination."

"I touched it," Faith said. "But only by the edges."

Avis wiggled her fingers. "I grabbed the letter before I saw what it was, so you'll need to take mine."

"I'll send someone up with the kit." Garris made a few notes. "One more thing. I'd like to speak to your assistant, Taylor Milner."

Faith's pulse leaped. *Is Taylor a suspect? She was out and about early the morning Avis was hit.*

Avis seemed to share Faith's suspicion, for she lurched, banging her elbow on the chair arm. She rubbed her elbow, wincing. "Why? What has she done? Did she run me over?"

Now Garris winced. "I can't discuss that." He glanced at Charlotte. "Isn't Miss Milner staying here?"

Charlotte opened her mouth to answer, but Avis spoke first. "Not anymore." She crossed her arms over her chest with a smirk. "I fired her this morning."

Watson, who had been watching from his position next to Faith, growled deep in his throat.

He doesn't like her either. "Hush, Rumpy," she whispered.

"So you did fire Taylor? I didn't want to believe it." Charlotte shook her head. "She's a fine young woman, so why on earth—?"

Avis picked up a pen and twiddled it. "I had to. She was poaching a client."

"Surely not." Charlotte looked appalled. "I can't picture her doing that."

"Well, she did." Avis's expression was that of a sulky toddler.

"I can help you locate Taylor, Chief Garris," Faith said, volunteering for the thankless task. Thankless on Taylor's end, anyway. She started to say that she was staying with Brooke, but she didn't want to give Avis any ammunition or information about her former assistant. "Brooke will know where she is."

"That would be much appreciated," Garris said. "And I'd like to talk to Eban Matthews right away also." He tucked away his notepad. "You mentioned he's working on the grounds today?"

Charlotte's skin went slightly green, and she clutched at her chest. "Eban? I thought he had been cleared."

Before the chief could answer, Avis slapped her hand on the table, her mouth dropping open. "Are you saying the gardener did it after all? How predictable. If this was a client's book, I'd send it back for rewrites."

Garris regarded Avis with disfavor. "As I said before, I can't discuss it. This is an ongoing investigation with routine inquiries. Please don't make any assumptions of guilt."

Charlotte exhaled in a sigh. "I'm glad Eban isn't in trouble. He's a good young man."

The agent was unabashed. "Hurry up and arrest someone, will you?"

Before the chief could blow his top, Faith intervened. "Let's go downstairs and find Brooke and Eban."

Charlotte walked them into the hallway. "Chief, I want to assure you that you have my full cooperation and that of my staff. Please let me know if you need anything."

He tipped his hat. "I appreciate that, Mrs. Jaxon. Have a good day."

"I'll be right back, Charlotte," Faith said. She made a rueful face. "Our work this morning keeps getting interrupted."

Wolfe's mother made a shooing motion. "Go on. This is far more important." She smiled. "I'll work on lunch for you and Wolfe."

Watson rubbed against Charlotte's ankles, purring.

"And Watson."

Lunch with Wolfe and his mother. Faith allowed her mind to wander a little while she led Chief Garris down to the basement level.

At the kitchen doorway, he said, "Please go in and get her. I don't want to disrupt meal preparations."

"She'll appreciate that." So for the second time that day, Faith entered the kitchen searching for Brooke. This time she found her up to her elbows in flour, kneading bread.

"Sorry to barge in again," Faith said when Brooke noticed her. "Chief Garris is here, looking for Taylor."

Brooke's eyes widened. "Taylor? Why?" She flipped the lump of dough and pummeled it on the other side.

Realizing that other people in the kitchen were listening, Faith lowered her voice. "I have no idea. Can you come out into the hallway for a minute?"

"If I must." Brooke grabbed a cloth and threw it over the bread, then followed Faith out of the kitchen.

"Thanks for letting me interrupt your work," Chief Garris said to Brooke. "I promise it won't take long. I need to find Taylor Milner immediately."

Brooke opened her mouth, and Faith could tell she wanted to ask questions. But instead she said, "She's sitting in the garden, writing. She decided to wait for me to get off work before heading over to my place."

At least going out to the garden would bring them closer to Eban's location. "Any idea where exactly?" Faith asked.

Brooke shook her head. "She didn't say." She wiped floury hands on her apron. "Shall I try to call her?"

"No, don't bother. I'll find her." Faith knew every nook and cranny of the gardens, having explored them with Watson.

Faith's first stop was a charming enclave that featured fragrant white roses and a tiny gazebo perfectly sized for one or two people. Seashells defined the walkways and marched along the gazebo railings. It was a wonderful spot to sit and work in privacy.

As she had hoped, Taylor was sitting in the gazebo, typing away on her laptop. She was so engrossed that she didn't even notice their arrival until they stood directly in front of her.

"Faith. Chief Garris." Taylor rose from her seat. "Is everything okay? Brooke? My parents?"

"I'm sorry to startle you, Miss Milner," Garris said. "I simply wanted to have a word."

"Whew." She plopped down again. Faith started to edge away, but Taylor said, "Stay, Faith. I have no secrets from you. Or my cousin." She smiled at Garris. "Go ahead, shoot."

The chief's face twisted in what was almost a smile. "Close. We've learned that you hold a license to carry firearms in this state."

Taylor's pale brows rose, almost touching her bangs. "So? Target shooting is one of my hobbies." She frowned in concern. "They didn't change the law or anything, did they?"

"No, you're all legal. But we did find your prints in Eban Matthews's car."

10

The pieces fell together for Faith. That's right. *They take finger-prints when people apply for gun permits. Was Taylor driving when her boss was hit? Her former boss, that is.* She held her breath waiting for Taylor's reply, hoping she was innocent.

The young woman cocked her head, puzzled. Then she laughed. "Oh yeah. I took Eban's car to get pizza the other night. Eban, Luis, Kate, Ivy, and I were all hanging out together, and my car was blocked in."

"When was that?" Garris wrote down the date and time Taylor mentioned. "Thank you. We'll be in touch."

When he turned away, ready to move on, Taylor gave Faith a questioning look behind his back.

Faith shrugged in response. It looked like Taylor was off the hook for now. *As long as her story checks out.*

"If you're searching for Eban," Faith said as she caught up with the chief, "we need to listen for the sound of lawn mowers."

They strolled along the path, soon catching the buzzing sound of an engine in the distance. After rounding a hedge, they saw Eban driving a riding mower on the spacious lawn near the maze. Head bent, he concentrated on his task as he motored back and forth.

Chief Garris chose a path that would intercept Eban on the next pass.

Spotting them, the gardener shut off the motor and pulled his headphones down around his neck. "Morning," he called, his eyes wary.

"I'll leave you, Chief," Faith said, wanting to be discreet. She walked toward the house, glancing over her shoulder to see the two men deep in conversation, Garris jotting notes.

Then Eban started the engine again, and the chief strode across the grass toward the parking lot. He waved to Faith.

Although she was dying to find out what the chief had said to Eban, she kept walking toward the manor. The sound of the mower grew louder, and she turned to see Eban driving her way. He cut the engine and leaped off in one lithe move.

"What did he want?" Faith asked. "If you don't mind me asking."

Eban shook his head, his gaze on the nearby border filled with daisies and daylilies. "He basically wanted to know who's been in my car over the past few months, specifically women." He grinned. "I told him he might need another notebook."

"You didn't." Faith couldn't hold back a laugh.

"I did." Eban lifted one shoulder and let it drop. "You have to keep a sense of humor, right?"

"It certainly helps." Faith deliberately kept her tone light. "Anyone I know?"

"Taylor, Ivy, Kate . . ." Eban ticked off names on his fingers, some of which were unfamiliar to Faith. "But lest you think I'm some kind of Casanova, we're all just friends."

Faith could understand that. When she was Eban's age, she and a gang of friends had rambled around town, staying at each other's apartments and sharing belongings, food, and even money sometimes.

"Do you know why the chief asked about that?" Faith asked. "Did he say?"

"I think he wants to eliminate some of the fingerprints." He studied his hands, front and back. "They already took mine."

"They're hoping to find those of the person who stole your car." *Unless Taylor or Ivy is guilty.* "How did the thief start the car? I know it's difficult to hot-wire many vehicles now. And I for one wouldn't know how."

Eban looked sheepish. "I leave the spare key under the mat. It's an old beater, and I honestly never thought anyone would steal it."

Or try to commit murder with it.

"This is the life," Wolfe said. "Sitting out here on the terrace with two lovely ladies in the sunshine, watching sailboats in the bay . . ." His voice trailed off, and he smiled at his mother and Faith. His blue eyes, so often steely and intense, were warm with laughter.

Faith speared a piece of avocado with her fork, wishing she could settle the butterflies in her belly. She'd shared plenty of meals with Wolfe, but this intimate lunch with him and his mother, high above the Castleton grounds, felt different. As if she'd been admitted to the inner Jaxon circle.

The food was lovely—a spring greens salad adorned with goat cheese, smoked salmon, tomatoes, and cucumbers, along with the avocado. Warm rolls and lemonade completed the menu, and a lemon chiffon custard awaited them for dessert.

"Castleton is certainly at its best this time of year," Charlotte remarked. "The gardens are looking better than ever."

"I'm glad you think so," Wolfe said. "We've got a wonderful crew of experts who treat this place like it's their own. I think they take real pride in making it as beautiful as it can be."

From this vantage point, the gardens spread out like an intricate and gorgeous mosaic. Faith's gaze roamed over her favorite spots. A familiar black-and-white figure caught her eye. There was Watson, poking about the herb garden. The gardeners always planted catnip for the manor's feline guests, and Watson must be seeking a treat.

The cat padded along the grassy path, drawn by the smell of his favorite treat. Well, one of his favorites, anyway. Those tunaroons were

something special, but his human had been rather remiss lately and had forgotten to buy more.

But no matter. The plant they called catnip would do just fine. The cat thrust his nose into the leafy patch, then plopped down and rolled, waving his paws in the air. Fortunately no one was around to witness this undignified abandon.

He lay on his back and blinked, watching birds soar through the blue sky. He waved a paw at one, but it only flapped away.

Moving side to side, he wiggled deeper into the plants. Something bit into his back. He flipped over and pushed at the greenery. The shiny object glinted in the sunlight. What fun! He pushed it out of the dirt. It landed on the rocky path, where it made a nice tinkling sound.

With a cry of satisfaction, he pounced.

"What's Watson got down there?" Wolfe asked, observing the cat with amusement.

Faith rose from her seat to get a better look. "I have no idea." The object caught the sun, reflecting a ray of light. "It's something shiny." She edged away from the table with a sigh. "I'd better go see in case it's something sharp. I don't want Watson to hurt himself."

"Bring him back with you," Charlotte said. "I'll make some coffee while you're gone." She smiled at her son. "Why don't you go down with Faith? Stretch your legs?"

Wolfe agreed, and they made their way down to the herb garden. By the time they arrived, Watson had tired of his game and was stretched out in the catnip, eyes closed.

"What did you find, old boy?" Wolfe bent to stroke his chin.

Faith searched around in the garden, gently moving the foliage aside, releasing scents of sage, oregano, and basil. "Here it is." She picked up the object. "It looks like a car key." She brushed dirt off it. Letters and an emblem were barely visible.

Wolfe took it from her and examined it front and back. "A key to an older make and model, that's for sure. Keys to new cars are electronic."

A thrill ran down Faith's spine. She knew of one car that fit the bill perfectly. "Do you suppose it belongs to Eban?"

"There's only one way to find out." Wolfe's handsome face set in grim lines.

The key sat on the table all through dessert, which Faith barely tasted. Between proximity to Wolfe and then possible evidence, the entire meal had been wasted, she realized ruefully.

"I'll find Eban this afternoon and ask him about this," Wolfe said. "No point in calling the police. That key might have sat in the garden for twenty years, buried in the dirt."

"There's a jazz trio scheduled for four o'clock," Charlotte said. "Why don't you wait until then? Oren and Luis are playing golf this afternoon, and Eban is caddying for them. You can't exactly ride out on the course to find him."

"Well, I could." Wolfe drummed his fingers on the table. "But you're right. I might as well wait."

Charlotte looked at her watch. "Faith and I have to interview models for the fashion show in a few minutes. That won't take long, so we can all ride out to the club together."

Wolfe's lip curled in amusement. "So much for your day of rest, Mother."

She raised a brow. "It's hard to keep a good woman down."

"That went well," Charlotte said as Wolfe, at the wheel of his BMW sedan, motored down the country club drive. "I'm so glad Kate Foster rounded up her friends for us."

"They'll be wonderful," Faith agreed. Kate had brought a gang of young men and women to Castleton that afternoon to audition as models. Leggy and lithe, they would wear the vintage styles with flair.

"Lorraine is working on a commentary for us," Charlotte said. "She and the other ladies are already here. They gathered earlier for lunch."

"Even Avis?" Faith asked. The woman could barely hobble, but she certainly seemed determined to get around.

Charlotte bit her lip. "Even Avis. No listening to doctor's orders for her."

Wolfe glanced in the rearview mirror at Faith, his eyes glinting with laughter. "That sounds familiar, doesn't it?"

"I plead the fifth," Faith said.

"Good answer." Charlotte gave her son a mock glare.

When they pulled up under the portico, a valet jogged down the steps to open the doors for them. "I'll park it for you, Mr. Jaxon," he offered.

Wolfe tossed him the keys. "Thank you." He gave the young man a generous tip.

Charlotte led them around the porch to the back terrace, where Lorraine and Avis had commandeered a large table. Most of the other tables were filled with laughing, chattering guests. In one corner, the jazz trio played smooth yet lively notes, a perfect accompaniment to the lovely afternoon.

After saying hello to Lorraine and Avis, Wolfe said, "Please excuse me. I'm going to visit the pro shop. I have an appointment to look at clubs."

As he strode away, Faith and Charlotte joined the other two at the table.

"Where is everybody?" Charlotte asked. She ordered two iced teas from a nearby server.

Lorraine swirled her straw in her glass. "Hildegarde is at the pool. Oren and Luis should be done with their round of golf by now, but they haven't shown up yet."

"I saw my ex-employee flitting around the grounds," Avis said, her expression even more sour than usual. "I'm surprised they let her in."

Charlotte settled her napkin on her lap. "Now, Avis, that's not a nice thing to say."

Avis smirked. "I know. I can't help myself sometimes." She snapped her fingers at the server, then pointed at her empty glass.

He rolled his eyes but brought her a fresh glass of tea when he delivered the ones Charlotte had ordered.

"I saw that," Avis told him. "Keep it up, and I'll go to the manager."

The server went pale and stuttered an apology.

Squirming at the woman's rudeness, Faith sent him a sympathetic smile.

"You'll do no such thing, Avis," Charlotte said sternly. To the hapless server, she said, "Thank you. Please come back in ten minutes, and we'll order appetizers."

"I'll do that, ma'am." Holding the tray up like a shield, he backed away, then turned and fled.

"I prefer Kate. Or Ivy. *They* know how to wait on tables." Avis ripped open three packets of sugar and dumped them into her glass of tea.

Too bad sugar doesn't sweeten a person's disposition. Wishing she had stayed home, Faith idly checked her phone. A missed call from her aunt. No message, which meant no emergency, but she decided to use it as an excuse. Waving her phone at the others, she rose from her chair. "Please excuse me. I need to make a call."

They merely nodded and continued their conversation, which had veered to identifying the tune the trio was playing.

The song was spirited, and Faith found herself almost breaking out into dance steps as she walked. She went around the corner of the porch to a quiet spot where a line of rockers sat. She chose one and scrolled through her phone to bring up Eileen's contact information.

She was about to press the button when a woman screamed.

11

Faith leaped out of the rocker, sending the chair swinging wildly. She hesitated, wondering where the scream had come from.

Then it pealed out again, a shriek that ripped through the tranquility of the warm afternoon. Something had happened on the terrace.

Faith dashed around the corner, hoping and praying that nothing terrible had occurred. But people don't scream unless . . .

Faith lurched to a stop, her T-strap sandals sliding on the painted boards.

Avis Roth sat slumped in her seat, her face resting on the tablecloth. Charlotte and Lorraine stood by the table, wearing horrified expressions. Lorraine was the screamer.

Charlotte snapped out of her stupor and bent over Avis. She pressed two fingers to her neck, then shook her head. "Call 911! Somebody! Anybody!"

A flurry broke out as diners and even the band grabbed their phones and began tapping.

"I got through," a man in golf apparel yelled. He talked self-importantly into the phone.

Marvin Treadwell, the manager, bustled out onto the terrace, forehead creased in concern, his head swiveling back and forth. He spotted the trouble and rushed over. "What's happened?" He bent close to Avis, then recoiled. "Is she ill?"

Faith wondered that herself. Had Avis succumbed to injuries from her accident? She'd heard of that happening—a clean bill of health but then suddenly someone was dead.

"She was hit by a golf ball," Charlotte said through tight lips. She shivered, pulling her cardigan closer around her shoulders.

"See? It's on the table." Lorraine flapped her hands at the white orb resting in the bowl of lemon slices.

At the news that a stray ball had severely injured a guest, the manager's face went gray. "Er, I'd better—uh, did anyone call 911?" When Marvin learned help was en route, his eyes brightened. "Maybe she'll make a full recovery."

"I couldn't find a pulse." Charlotte shivered again, clutching at her sweater, and Faith realized she was going into shock.

Faith pushed through several onlookers to the woman's side. "Come on, Charlotte. Let's sit down." She guided her to another table that was well away from Avis. After getting her settled, she waved at the server. "Hot tea, with lots of sugar, please."

He didn't seem to hear, so she repeated her request.

He finally tore his attention away from the hubbub. "Right away, ma'am." He scuttled toward the door, bumping into other onlookers coming the other way.

Wolfe came running around the corner of the building. "What happened? I heard—" He stopped when he saw Avis. "Oh no. How terrible." He went to his mother's side and rested a hand on her shoulder. "Perhaps I should take you home."

"Not yet," Charlotte snapped. "I need to talk to the police." She drew herself up in the chair. "I'm a witness."

He scratched his head. "But surely it was an accident."

Charlotte snorted. "Of course. But they'll still take statements."

"You're right. I guess I'm not thinking clearly." Wolfe's eyes were deep pools of concern as he gazed at his mother.

Faith could sympathize with his desire to take Charlotte away from the scene. If she hadn't been involved with the tragedy, Faith would have been heading for the exit herself. Unlike many of the people here, Faith did not take pleasure in rubbernecking. Word must have spread, for now carts were tootling in from the course, heading right toward the clubhouse instead of to their berth near the pro shop.

Marvin conferred with a couple of staff members and sent them out to intercept the carts.

The sound of sirens was heard, steadily growing louder as the vehicles raced toward the scene.

Wolfe straightened his shoulders and forced his way through the crowd to Marvin's side. After a few words with the manager, he returned to the deck. With a sharp whistle, he caught the crowd's attention. Projecting his voice with the natural poise and presence of a leader, Wolfe said, "An ambulance and the police are on their way. Everyone, please go inside and wait, in case the police want to talk to you." He addressed a nearby server. "Please keep them all hydrated and fed and put it on my tab."

The bystanders moved in a throng toward the entrance doors.

Thundering footsteps announced the arrival of the EMTs, who obviously knew the outside route was shorter than going through the building.

Lorraine took a seat beside Charlotte.

"Would you like tea?" Faith asked, her hand hovering over the pot.

The other woman waved away her offer. "Not right now." She shuddered. "A couple of inches to the right and that ball would have hit *me*."

"It could just as easily have hit me too." Charlotte's tone was somber.

Faith thought of something. "Where's Oren? And Luis? Aren't they here somewhere?"

Lorraine watched as the EMTs examined Avis. "I'm not sure. Perhaps they're still playing golf."

One of the EMTs shook his head. "She's gone," he told the other in a low tone.

Charlotte overheard and moaned, her brittle self-possession slipping away.

"How awful!" Lorraine shrieked. She put both hands over her face and sobbed.

Poor Avis. How quickly death could come, striking out of nowhere. Faith's heart felt heavy with grief. The loss of life was terrible, no matter how unpleasant the person had been.

The sound of voices and laughter grated on Faith's ear. When she glanced over, she spotted Eban and Taylor wandering along one of the gravel paths, headed right for the terrace.

She needed to stop them, to protect Taylor from the shock of seeing Avis's body. Without a word to anyone, Faith skirted the empty tables and flew down the steps to the lawn. As she ran down the path, she saw Chief Garris and Officer Laddy arrive on the scene.

Eban noticed Faith first, giving her a friendly wave. "Are you enjoying the afternoon? It's a beauty."

Faith bit her lip. There was no easy way to say it. She took a deep, steadying breath, pushing down the nausea that threatened to rise. "Taylor, I'm afraid I have some bad news."

Horror descended over the young woman's face. "B-Brooke?" she stuttered.

"No, not Brooke," Faith said with haste. "Avis. A golf ball hit her . . . and I'm afraid she's dead."

Taylor gave a little scream. Her knees buckled, and Eban hurried to prop her up. "Avis is dead? I can't believe it." She buried her face in his shoulder and began to cry.

"Let's go back to the terrace," Faith said. "The chief will probably want to talk to you. To all of us," she amended.

The trio shuffled along, Eban helping Taylor, who seemed to have lost proper use of her legs.

Chief Garris was ushering the witnesses around the corner to the side porch where Faith had tried to call her aunt. Other officers had arrived and were investigating the area. Faith knew that the medical examiner would soon be here to examine Avis before she would mercifully be removed from the public eye.

By the time they climbed the steps to the side porch, Chief Garris was questioning Charlotte and Lorraine while Officer Laddy took notes. Oren and Luis had arrived and stood listening nearby, along with Wolfe. He greeted Faith with a nod of approval when he saw she had informed Taylor.

"We were drinking tea and enjoying the jazz when I heard a pop, and then Avis fell face-first onto the table." Again Charlotte tugged at her sweater. "She didn't move." She took a deep, shuddering breath. "And I couldn't find a pulse."

"That's exactly right," Lorraine said. "I heard that sound too and wondered what it was. It must have been the ball hitting her." She took a deep breath. "Then the ball bounced once on the tablecloth and landed in the bowl of lemons." She demonstrated the ball's movement.

Oren moved closer to his wife. "I'm grateful it didn't hit you, my dear."

She smiled at him and took his hand.

Garris stood, hands on hips. "Can you get me the names of the golfers on the course when it happened?" he asked Marvin.

"Yes." Marvin wrung his hands. "We'll do everything we can to cooperate with the police. But it won't be easy to determine whose ball hit her. They frequently go wild, especially when you have golfers of all abilities."

"Get me the list," Garris ordered.

The manager marched off like a man on a mission.

Garris swung around to face the others. "I'd like to find out where the rest of you were when the incident happened." He pointed to the doors behind them, the outside entrance to the private dining room. "One at a time."

Lorraine squeezed her husband's hand. "You don't really think any of them had something to do with what happened?"

"I was in the pro shop looking at clubs," Oren said with a laugh. "That takes care of me."

The chief's retort was sharp. "I gather information, and then I think."

A regal figure dressed in a caftan and a turban strolled along the path from the pool. Noticing the gathering on the porch, Hildegarde diverted her route. She paused at the foot of the steps. "What's going on?"

"Oh, Hildy, something horrible has happened!" Lorraine cried.

Before Hildegarde could ask any questions, Charlotte jumped in. "Poor Avis has had a terrible accident. She's dead."

Hildegarde gasped. "Dead? But I was only at the pool an hour." She put a hand to her forehead and swayed slightly.

With lithe movements, Luis crossed the porch and took her elbow. He assisted her up the stairs and to a rocking chair.

Chief Garris greeted her and filled her in. "I'd like to speak to you as well, Mrs. Maxwell."

Her face was a pale oval under the turban. "Whatever I can do to help."

"I'll start with you, Mr. Jaxon," Garris said. He opened the door of the dining room and ushered Wolfe inside. The glass-paned door rattled shut behind them.

The group waiting on the porch sat in stony-faced silence. Faith looked around the circle. After initial bursts of dismay, not much sorrow had been expressed. But perhaps they were all still numb.

Oren broke the silence with a bark of dry laughter. "It's an ill wind that blows no good. Forgive my use of cliché, a writer's last refuge. But face it, folks. Not one of us sitting here is worse off than we were an hour ago." He shook his head. "A sad commentary on a life poorly lived."

The group attending the presentation by Oren and Luis that evening at the manor was unusually subdued. The loss of Avis cast a pall, not only for the shock of her sudden death but the absence of her bold personality. Faith realized that for all Avis's faults, the woman had

had a way of sharpening the conversation and wits of those around her, if only because others had been trying to escape her cruel tongue.

After mingling for a while, the group was seated, with Oren and Luis sitting casually at the front of the room on a small dais.

Charlotte introduced them. "We are fortunate tonight to have two of our country's leading literary lights. Each has been called a voice of his generation in the vein of the legendary F. Scott Fitzgerald, whom we celebrate this week."

There was a brief burst of applause.

"Without further ado, I leave you in the capable hands of Oren Edwards and Luis Gerardo." Charlotte stepped aside.

The clapping was now thunderous, accompanied by the stamping of feet and whistles.

Faith noticed Taylor and Lorraine sitting together, their faces pink with pride as they gazed upon the men they loved.

The audience finally settled, but before either of the men could speak, a redheaded woman popped up in the back. Faith recognized her as a tabloid reporter she'd dealt with before. "Is it true that Avis Roth, one of New York's finest literary agents, was murdered today?"

Everyone turned to look at her and then began to talk, whispering that soon built to a wave of murmuring.

Charlotte, the line between her brows revealing her annoyance, stepped up to the front of the room. "I'm sorry, miss, but this is neither the time nor the place." She gestured to Castleton staff lining the back wall. "Please escort this young lady out."

The reporter didn't seem happy, but she allowed the men to guide her out of the room. She made sure she got in a parting shot, though. "Ask your police chief. He'll be seeking an indictment."

12

The reporter's comment raised a ruckus in the room, and the murmuring became a deafening roar.

Faith's heart was racing. Was the woman telling the truth? Had someone deliberately hit Avis with the golf ball? But surely such an accurate shot was almost impossible.

And if Chief Garris suspected someone, who was it? One of the men Avis had refused to represent—Eban or Luis? Her unhappy client Oren? Or Taylor, the assistant she'd brutally fired?

Faith's head spun as she considered each possibility. Then, with a few deep breaths, calm descended. No doubt the reporter was seeking to stir the pot. There had been no hint that Chief Garris was considering murder charges that afternoon. True, he'd questioned everyone, but that was standard protocol.

Charlotte put two fingers in her mouth and whistled. "All right, everyone. Now that our fifteen minutes of fame are over, let's return to our program."

The audience roared in appreciative laughter.

Charlotte welcomed Oren and Luis back to the stage.

Oren started off with a moment of silence for Avis, a graceful touch. Then he spoke briefly of her work as his agent and her guidance in building his career. Now that Avis was gone, he seemed almost nostalgic about the woman, seeming to forget that she had been critical of his latest book.

Luis lightened the mood with a remark that she'd rejected him, but somehow fortune had smiled on him and he had done well. His modest understatement brought down the house. He thanked his mother, who had sacrificed for him so he could have a great education, one that, as he put it, "had made all the difference."

Not to be outdone, Oren gave a shout-out to his wife, who preened when the spotlight focused on her.

After that introduction, they swung into the presentation. They used an informal style, bantering back and forth, trading notes and observations. Faith was captivated by this inside look into the minds of two famous writers. Then the men opened the discussion for questions from the crowd.

Brooke sidled up to Faith, who was standing against the back wall. "Hey," she whispered. "Pretty good, huh?"

"Fascinating," Faith whispered back.

Oren took a final question, and the session wrapped up. People pushed back their chairs with scraping sounds and stood in small clusters to chat.

"Chief Garris was just here," Brooke said.

Faith's heart lurched. "Was he making an arrest?" It couldn't have been Taylor he was apprehending because she stood beside Luis, her arm through his, glowing with happiness.

Brooke leaned closer and whispered, "No. He sealed Avis's room. What do you suppose that means?"

"You know what it means. They think Avis was murdered."

A woman nearby sent them an odd look, and Faith wondered if she'd overheard. She suppressed a pang of guilt at speaking without thinking, especially so loudly. Nothing could squash that kind of news. It was only a matter of hours before the whole world knew.

Taylor and Luis had been making their way through the sea of guests, stopping frequently for the exchange of greetings. They reached Faith and Brooke.

"Guess what?" Taylor said, her blue eyes sparkling with joy. "Luis and I just got engaged!"

Brooke squealed and flung herself into her cousin's arms. "That's wonderful news!"

"Congratulations." Faith smiled at the couple. "I'm thrilled for you both."

"What an amazing turn of events, especially after the horrible day you've had," Brooke said.

"I know." Taylor's tone was fervent. "This morning I was ready to curl up and die, and tonight I'm floating on air."

Luis put an arm around his future bride and pulled her close. "I suggested she take a position with my literary agent's company, but she wants to strike out on her own."

"Really?" Brooke's expression was one of surprise and admiration. "That's brave of you, working for yourself."

Taylor's cheeks flushed. "I'm not starting from scratch. I'm lining up a couple of solid clients to begin with. Then I'll go from there."

A familiar figure in blue made his way through the crowd. Chief Garris nodded at the little group. "Miss Milner, I'd like a word."

"Of course." Taylor sent her fiancé a worried look.

Luis tightened his grip on Taylor's hand, threaded through his arm. "Want me to come with you, babe?"

"I need to speak to her alone," Garris said. "It will only take a moment."

"Do I need a lawyer?" Taylor's laugh was strained. "Wait for me, Luis. I'll be right back."

Faith watched the small, brave figure follow the chief out of the room. Avis had hurt Taylor terribly while she was alive. Now the young woman was poised for happiness, both personal and professional, and Faith hoped the agent's death wouldn't hurt Taylor even more.

"The police found a list in Avis's room," Taylor told the assembled ladies at the emergency meeting of the book club the next morning. "She was calling people in New York to blackball me." She wiped away tears. "Fortunately, she only made it partway through the list."

Midge gasped. "That's just horrible. I can't believe she'd do such a thing. I didn't notice that when I went to the room to fetch poor Fitz." Midge had taken the ferret to her boarding facility until Avis's cousin arrived to claim him.

"It was bad enough she fired you. But to go to that extreme? Downright evil." Brooke dabbed away powdered sugar left by the beignet she was munching. She'd been able to attend the meeting because a continental breakfast was being served at Castleton and other staff could handle it.

"So the police think she was murdered?" Eileen's tone was thoughtful. "The odds of a golf ball hitting someone and killing them are extremely high. They'd have to be a phenomenal golfer."

"That lets me off the hook," Taylor said. "I can't even hit a golf ball. I just make divots."

"I guess after the hit-and-run accident they're being extra cautious." Faith pulled out a pad of paper and a pen. "Let's go through this one step at a time. We know a woman was driving the car."

"Yeah, and my fingerprints are all over the wheel." Taylor's blue eyes widened. "I feel like a character in one of Oren's books. 'I've been framed.'"

"The hit-and-run accident actually reminds me of *The Great Gatsby*," Eileen said. "And someone is killed by a car in Luis's book."

Brooke tilted her head. "That's right. Do you think he consciously put it in there?"

"Maybe," Eileen said. "Sometimes authors give nods to literary greats by including bits and pieces that echo the famous work."

"Speaking of plot twists, do you think we have one killer or two?" Midge set Atticus—who was snuggled on her lap—on the floor and went to the refreshment table. She picked up the coffee carafe. "Anyone else want a refill?"

Eileen held out her cup. "That's an interesting thought, Midge."

"It might be the only thing that makes sense," Brooke said. "Two different people."

Faith accepted a serving of hot coffee. "I'm going to list all the people who knew Avis in two columns and then note where they were during the crimes. Chime in with what you know." She set her mug down and grabbed her pen.

"Let's start with who we know is innocent," Brooke said. "Charlotte Jaxon. She was at the table when Avis was hit by the golf ball, right?"

"Yes," Faith said. "And I assume in the apartment when Avis was hit by a car."

"How about Lorraine Edwards and Hildegarde Maxwell?" Brooke asked.

Faith wrote them down. "During the hit-and-run accident, Lorraine was at Castleton, we think, but she was sitting with Avis yesterday. The day of the car accident, Hildegarde was at the drugstore. I saw her return to the manor. Yesterday she was at the pool."

"How about Ivy Maxwell?" Taylor suggested. She shivered. "It's awful casting suspicion on your friends."

"I know," Midge said, "but unfortunately it's part of the process." Atticus snuffled around her shoes, and she leaned down to rub his ears.

"Does anyone know where Ivy was the morning of the car accident?" Faith asked.

Everyone shook their heads.

"What about yesterday?" Faith continued.

"I saw her at the country club," Taylor admitted. "She was pushing a bin of fresh towels to the pool."

"I was wondering about that." Faith paused to sip coffee. "She wasn't working the dining room."

Taylor waved a hand. "Don't forget about me. I went for a run the morning Avis was hit, and when the golf ball struck her, I was talking to Eban." Her cheeks reddened at this admission.

Brooke gave her cousin a questioning look.

Taylor quickly added, "About his book. I want to sign him as one of my first clients."

Warmth filled Faith's heart. "That's wonderful, Taylor. His book is spectacular. I could never understand why Avis wouldn't represent him."

"Me neither." Taylor crossed her arms with a frown. "She was adamant that she didn't want to take him on. But she read the whole manuscript. I saw her."

"That's unusual, right?" Midge commented. "Not that I know anything about literary agents, but why would she waste her time? She must have been inundated with books to read."

"Very strange." Faith made a note of that. "Back to the country club. If Eban was talking to you, then he must have been done caddying for Oren and Luis."

Taylor nodded. "I intercepted them all when they returned to the clubhouse. Oren and Luis took off somewhere, and Eban and I went for a walk."

"I hate to do this, but they both need to go on the list," Faith said. "Let's try to get more details about where Oren and Luis were."

"Luis had nothing to do with it," Taylor protested. "He didn't like Avis, but why would he kill her?"

Good question. "I'm sorry, Taylor," Faith said. "But we have to check out everyone and then try to clear them one by one."

"Maybe Luis saw something yesterday," Brooke said. "You never know."

Taylor brightened. "That's true. He's very observant, like most writers."

Faith thought of someone else she needed to question. *Wolfe.* He'd been at the club.

"Where was the stolen car left?" Eileen asked. "Maybe that would tell us something."

"Eban mentioned it," Taylor said. She thought for a moment, then named a dead-end street on the fringe of town.

"Hmm. That's interesting." Eileen went to her office and brought back a town map, which she unrolled on a table. The others gathered around. She traced the short lane with a forefinger. "This is where the police found the abandoned car."

"Look," Faith said. "That street dead-ends in woods bordering public land and eventually Castleton's grounds."

"Maybe someone left the car there and hiked back to the manor," Brooke suggested. "There's a path through those woods."

"That's a possibility, but you can also get downtown from there pretty easily." Midge stabbed at the residential and shopping area right next to the street in question.

"Very true," Eileen said. "The location isn't as conclusive as one might hope."

Faith sighed. "It's another piece of the puzzle. Hopefully they'll all fall into place soon."

"There you are." Charlotte took Faith aside as she entered the Great Hall Gallery. "We lost a model. Poor Audrey is sick with a cold."

"You want me to find someone else?" Faith asked, noticing that the chairs in front of the catwalk were already filling up. "But aren't we starting in half an hour?"

"We are. And that's why I want you to fill in." Charlotte looked Faith up and down. "You're the right size, so Audrey's clothes will look good on you."

Faith was flabbergasted. "Me? Model?" The rest of the women involved were under twenty-five.

"Why not? She's making me do it." Wolfe joined their conversation. "Come on, Faith. It will be fun."

The addition of Wolfe to the escapade did change Faith's mind somewhat, almost making her forget her trepidation about prancing around in front of an audience. With Charlotte watching her, Faith felt the pressure of time quickly ticking away. Every moment, more people filtered into the room. Luis sat down at the piano and began to bang out bouncy ragtime, a signal that the curtain would soon go up. Lorraine was already at a podium to one side of the catwalk, glancing through her notes.

"All right," Faith finally said. "How can I say no?"

"Good decision," Wolfe said. "Now let's get to the dressing rooms."

The library had been transformed into the women's dressing room while the adjacent den served as the men's.

Wolfe opened the door to the den, pausing to give her a wink. "Break a leg."

"Oh, I undoubtedly will," she said. She wasn't known for her grace under fire.

Inside the library, all was bedlam. Hairdressers and makeup artists were getting the models ready, and other women stood by to help them dress. Marlene supervised the chaos with her well-honed traffic-control skills. The time between vignettes was short, Charlotte had told Faith earlier, so it would be off with one outfit and on with the next, barely leaving time to breathe.

"Reporting for duty," Faith told the closest assistant.

"As what?" the woman asked, glancing down at her clipboard.

"I'm filling in for Audrey." Faith gave her a wry smile. "As a model."

Kate's head popped up from behind a rack of clothing. Kohl-lined eyes and bright red lipstick had transformed the college student into the very image of a flapper. "Faith, you're modeling? That's awesome." She rummaged through the racks. "Audrey's outfits are right here. Come see."

Faith joined Kate at the rack. The hangers were labeled with each model's name.

"You've got a tennis dress," Kate said. "A burgundy dress-and-coat outfit. Look, real fur on the collar. Do you believe they wore that? And finally, a slip dress for the evening vignette."

"It's gorgeous." Faith couldn't hold back a gasp at the last piece of clothing. The delicate dress shimmered with tiny beads. They adorned the neckline and hem and formed patterns on the sheer overskirt covering sea-green silk.

Kate was hunkered down, searching for shoes. "Hopefully these will fit." She stood and handed Faith a pair of black T-straps.

Faith examined the shoes. "They look fine. Good thing I'm the same size as Audrey."

"Otherwise you'd be hobbling or swimming," Kate said with a laugh.

Faith lowered her voice slightly. "I've been meaning to ask, any news about the missing items at the country club?"

Kate thrust out her bottom lip. "I'm afraid not. And a few more things have gone missing. A woman reported the loss of a gold necklace yesterday."

"That's awful. Is the manager going to do anything about it?"

"He said he has plans to." Kate rolled her eyes. "We'll see. In the meantime, I'm still looking for my grandmother's earrings. They haven't shown up yet, according to the police."

"Miss," one of the makeup artists called, crooking a finger at Faith, "come get your face on."

"That's my cue, I guess," Faith said, putting the shoes down. She hurried to the makeup area, which consisted of two chairs set up in front of a long mirror.

Ivy was in the other chair having her short hair crimped into marcel waves. She gave Faith an almost imperceptible nod of greeting, not moving her gaze from her reflection.

"Hi, Ivy. How have you been?" Faith asked after the makeup artist finished dabbing cleanser on her face. She'd hardly had a chance to talk to the young woman, let alone get to know her.

"I'm okay." Ivy shrugged one slender shoulder, earning a dirty look from the hairdresser, who had to step back with the hot iron. "Sorry," she told the woman. Her eyes met Faith's briefly in the mirror. "That was quite a shock yesterday about Avis Roth." She scrunched up her nose. "I'm sure glad I wasn't on dining room duty."

Rather a cold reaction, Faith thought. "Did you know her well? I had the impression she was friends with your grandmother." She held her face still as the artist stroked thick foundation base on her cheeks.

Ivy pouted her lips. "I'm not sure if they were exactly *friends*. I mean, Ms. Roth came to my grandparents' parties, but that's because Grandpa worked with her. He called her a necessary evil."

Interesting. Faith closed her eyes briefly as the artist patted her skin with a damp sponge. When she opened them again to check her reflection, she jumped.

Hildegarde was standing right behind her, staring intently at Faith's reflection in the mirror.

13

Faith's eyes met Hildegarde's for a long, fraught moment that sent a chill down her spine. *What is that all about? Did she hear us discussing Avis?*

Then Hildegarde regarded her granddaughter. "You look lovely, dear," she said, her austere features relaxing into a smile.

"Thanks, Nana." Ivy's expression didn't change. She continued to study her reflection in the glass. "Do you have some money I can borrow? I need to pay rent, and payday is next week."

Feeling intrusive, Faith dropped her gaze. But she did see the smile fade from the older woman's face, replaced by a crease of annoyance between her arched brows.

"I've told you before . . . Let's not discuss it now. I'll see you after the show." Hildegarde adjusted the beaded necklace she wore with her purple silk frock and strode away, her shoulders stiff and straight.

Ivy gave a little laugh and rolled her eyes. "Grandmothers. They can be such a pain sometimes. Isn't that right?"

The hairdresser, making one final tweak to Ivy's waves, didn't appear to hear.

Ivy flushed red, and when she noticed Faith watching her, she sent her a glare.

Faith quickly looked away, thankful when the makeup artist told her to close her eyes so she could apply shadow. When she opened them a minute later, Ivy had vacated her seat and another young woman was sitting there, having her long hair arranged in a bun.

A few minutes later, the ordeal of elaborate hair and makeup was over, and Faith was released to put on her first costume, the tennis dress. She even had a prop to carry, an old-fashioned wood racket.

The pairing of men and women put her with Wolfe, who was dashing in tennis whites. "Maybe we should try this in real life." He swished his racket with a grin. "But with modern equipment."

"Shh, all of you." Marlene's whisper was fierce. "It's time to go on." She stood in the wings, checking the list and confirming the couples were in the right order.

"Yes ma'am," Wolfe said, his eyes twinkling. "It won't happen again."

Faith stifled a smile. When it came to making sure events at Castleton went off without a hitch, even the lord of the manor wasn't immune to Marlene's scolding.

Onstage, Lorraine began her spiel. "Fashions of the 1920s were notable not only for their beauty but for the reflection of changing times and tastes. No longer were women hampered by ankle-length skirts and long sleeves while they engaged in sports. Sometimes they even wore knickers." Her voice dropped. "Scandalous."

The audience laughed.

At this cue, Kate strode onto the catwalk, wearing the jaunty knickers, vest, and white shirt once used as golf attire. She mugged for the crowd, waving one leg then the other, to more laughter.

Next was a model wearing Coco Chanel's famous beach pajamas, wide-legged pants worn while sailing.

Faith's heart pounded, and her palms dampened with sweat. Her turn was coming up, and she had no idea what to do. Why on earth had she agreed to do this?

"Follow my lead," Wolfe whispered, as if reading her mind. "I'm going to pretend to serve the ball to you."

They strolled side by side down the narrow section of the runway, and at the end, they parted. Wolfe served an invisible ball to her, and Faith reached out with her racket to lob it back. Comically he pretended to leap for it, only to miss, shaking his head.

The onlookers loved it, bursting into laughter and applause.

"Some things haven't changed," Lorraine said, picking up on the unscripted action. "Women still surprise men every day of the week."

That brought more applause and a few hoots.

Backstage again, Faith felt warmth flush her cheeks. "That wasn't so bad," she said. Wolfe's clowning had taken her mind off the fact that the audience was watching her every move.

"You did great," Wolfe said, patting her on the shoulder.

"No time to dawdle," Marlene barked. "Hurry up and change."

Faith scooted for the library, almost breaking into a run. She found her spot at the rack and shucked off the tennis dress, careful not to rip it. On with the dress, matching jacket, stockings, and shoes. She topped it off with a feathered cloche.

An attendant dashed over and twitched the outfit into place, then brushed down the sleeves.

Meanwhile, a small group had gone out to display uniforms worn at Castleton in the 1920s. Charlotte had dug them out of some trunks in the attic. When those models started to trickle back in, Faith went to the door.

"Aren't you elegant," Kate drawled, looking pretty spiffy herself in a green dress and coat. A peacock feather adorned her turban. She removed one of her ropes of false pearls and dropped it over Faith's head. "The finishing touch."

"Thanks." Faith played with the pearls, twining them in her fingers.

Wolfe joined her side, dapper in a pinstripe suit and fedora. He tipped the brim of his hat. "I might wear this to work next week. What do you think?"

"Very nice." Faith smiled at the thought of Wolfe wearing vintage clothing to his office in Boston.

"Face front. It's time." Marlene went down the line, pulling and pushing people into place. "Let's go. In time with the beat, if you please."

"I think she missed her calling," Wolfe whispered. He held out his elbow for Faith to take. "She should have been a drill sergeant."

"They thought she was too strict," Faith whispered back, "so she came here." She shared a grin with Wolfe, then set her face into the proper aloof lines for the parade.

"Ladies and gentlemen," Lorraine said, "next we have the Bon Voyage Collection. Travel burgeoned in the 1920s. More options at lower cost brought touring the United States or the Continent into the reach of the middle class."

Faith tried to project the demeanor of a woman setting off on a long sea voyage as she and Wolfe promenaded down the stage arm in arm. At the end, he swung into another skit, this time leaning close and pointing, as if showing her something out at sea. She pretended to respond with great interest.

Then she did notice something unusual on one of the balconies lining the two-story hall. Luis was skulking along against the wall, staying in the shadows.

She blinked, not sure she was seeing correctly. Wasn't Luis playing the piano? And if not, why was he being sneaky? Guests were allowed to roam Castleton.

Her assignment dictated she hold her head straight and look forward. That meant she wasn't able to indulge her curiosity and see who was noodling away at the keyboard. She had to wait until she and Wolfe turned to sashay down the catwalk and toward Lorraine at the podium. A short, rotund man sat at the piano, banging out peppy jazz. So it *was* Luis creeping around the hallway.

Faith had one more outfit to model, so she couldn't tear off upstairs and find out what was going on. The only positive result of this frustrating situation was that it took her mind off being onstage. The entire time she was changing into the gossamer green frock and prancing along the catwalk with Wolfe, who was devastating in his white tie and tails, she wondered what Luis was doing upstairs.

He returned as she and Wolfe descended the short flight of stairs behind the stage at the end of the fashion show. Instead of taking a seat or returning to the piano, the writer found a spot next to Taylor against the wall. She turned to speak to him, and in response, he shook his head.

"Would you join me for dinner?" Wolfe asked.

Faith tore her attention away from the couple and tried to focus on what Wolfe was saying. "You're asking me to dinner?" She hoped that she didn't look as foolish as she felt. Here was Wolfe extending an invitation, and she was too busy wondering what Luis was doing, which was probably nothing at all.

Wolfe chuckled. "Well, only the buffet." He held out his arm again. "Come with me?"

"I'd be delighted." She smiled and slid her hand into the crook of his elbow.

They made their way through the Great Hall Gallery, still filled with lingering guests. Every few feet, someone stopped them with a compliment or a comment. Wolfe's acting had been a hit, and many people assured Faith that she was stunning in the period clothing.

In the banquet hall, a buffet featuring prime rib and whole turkeys had been set up. Expert carvers sliced meat to order, and other staff made sure the vegetable selections were kept topped up.

Wolfe guided Faith to a seat at the head table and held out the chair for her. "What would you like? I'll fetch it for you."

Faith mentally reviewed the buffet offerings. She was starving. "That'd be great. Thanks. I'll have a slice of beef, Yorkshire pudding, potatoes, gravy, and a green vegetable, whatever they have." Immediately she wanted to bite her tongue. *Why didn't I just ask for a salad?* Wolfe's late fiancée had been a model. No doubt she'd existed on lettuce leaves and air.

He grinned. "Great plan. That's what I was going to get for myself. I'll be right back."

Carrying loaded plates, Oren and Lorraine made their way to the table and sat down across from Faith. They busied themselves arranging their meal, salting the food, and unwrapping silverware from napkins.

"You did a lovely job tonight, Faith," Lorraine said. "I understand you were a pinch hitter."

"Thank you. I was indeed. One of the models was sick." Faith accepted a server's offer to fill her glass with iced lemon water. She took a sip. "Your speech was fascinating."

Busy cutting her meat, Lorraine lifted a shoulder in acknowledgment. "I'm glad you enjoyed it. I love the 1920s. They were an intriguing time, full of glamour and life. Colorful. They don't make decades like that anymore, do they, dear?"

"Not since the '60s." Oren kept his head bent, intent on devouring his prime rib.

"Here we are." Wolfe set a plate in front of Faith, then another at the adjacent place. He sat and placed his napkin in his lap.

"What a nice gesture," Lorraine said, studying Wolfe and Faith with good-humored curiosity. "My husband used to do that for me, but after thirty years the honeymoon is over."

"How can you say that?" Oren demanded. "I brought you coffee in bed this morning. Or did you forget?"

Lorraine put a hand on his arm. "Of course not. And I appreciated it, as I do every day." She turned back to Faith. "I'm absolutely useless until I get my first cup of coffee in the morning. He brings it to me at eight o'clock sharp. Then I stay in bed and read for an hour."

The banter was light, but the truth behind the words gradually sank in. Lorraine was not an early riser. And Oren would have brought Lorraine her coffee after Avis had been hit by the car. Had he run out and done it while his wife was asleep? But a woman had been driving. . .

Charlotte and Hildegarde arrived at the table with their food. Charlotte sat next to Oren, and Hildegarde took the chair beside Wolfe.

"I can't wait to get behind the wheel," Hildegarde said to Charlotte. "I have a need for speed, as they say."

"Me too," Charlotte said. "Ten to one I beat you."

Faith suppressed a sigh when she remembered the car race at

Blake Jaxon's speedway was tomorrow. This week had been so busy. She longed for a quiet book retreat, marked only by guests clamoring for library recommendations.

"Mother, you're supposed to let your guests win," Wolfe objected.

"Balderdash," Charlotte declared. "It's no fun unless it's a fair race."

"That's the spirit," Oren said. "May the best woman win."

Lorraine gave her husband a sly smile. "Oh, didn't I tell you? I'm racing too. Charlotte found me a darling coupe to drive."

"A darling coupe with a souped-up engine," Charlotte said drily. She gave the engine specifications, which frankly were gibberish to Faith.

"Your mother is an amazing woman," she whispered to Wolfe.

"She is indeed." He grabbed his plate. "I'm heading up for seconds. Do you want anything?"

Faith noticed to her chagrin that her plate was almost licked clean. "No thanks. It was very good, though." She put a hand over her full belly. One good thing about dropped-waist dresses was that they didn't pinch after a full meal.

"Any news from those agents yet?" Lorraine asked her husband.

"No, but it looks encouraging. Several people are interested." Oren mopped up the gravy on his plate with a dinner roll.

"I still can't get over how Avis planned to drop you." Lorraine pressed her lips together. "I know they say not to speak ill of the dead, but I'm sure tempted."

"It was quite a blow, but I'm over it now." Oren popped the last piece of bread into his mouth. "I'm sure I'll find a new agent without a problem."

"They ought to snap you up." Lorraine's tone was tense. "You're one of the country's finest writers."

Listening in fascination to this conversation, Faith asked, "What's your new book about? If you don't mind sharing."

The couple exchanged looks and sheepish smiles.

"Well, it's not exactly funny under the circumstances," Oren said. "But it's a murder mystery about the death of a literary agent."

Faith couldn't hold back a surprised gulp of laughter. "Really? Maybe Avis thought literary agents should be off-limits in mysteries. As victims, that is." She didn't know if she'd relish reading about a murdered librarian.

"Could be," Oren said. "But none of the others I've spoken to seem to object to the plot. The book is clever, full of literary allusions."

The color drained from Lorraine's cheeks, and the expression on her face could only be called horrified. "Oren, don't you get it? They're hoping the publicity around Avis's death will give your book a boost. That's just awful." She pushed back her chair and fled from the room.

14

Faith stared after Lorraine in bewilderment.

Oren didn't turn a hair. "Don't mind my wife. She's a little excitable." He reached for another roll and the butter knife.

"Do you think she's right about the, um, interest in your book?" Faith bit her lip, wondering if she was being rude by asking.

"Perhaps. Who cares, as long as I get a good deal?" Oren winked. "Meaning five figures, if not six."

Faith shifted in her chair, uncomfortable with the man's bald pragmatism. Perhaps he was self-centered enough to use a tragedy to his advantage, bloodthirsty as that seemed. A thought struck like a thunderbolt, making her shiver. *Did he cause Avis's death in order to boost his book?*

Thankfully, Wolfe returned to the table at that moment.

"Sorry. I got hung up at the buffet table talking to someone." Wolfe sat beside Faith and settled his napkin back on his lap. "Where's Lorraine?"

"She stepped out." Oren's tone was placid. "But she'll be back soon."

Charlotte got up from the table and paused between Faith and Wolfe. "I'm heading upstairs. See you in the morning. Remember, the cars are leaving for the racetrack at eight o'clock."

"We'll be there," Wolfe said. "Good night, Mother."

The cat crept through the bushes, careful to stay out of sight. His person had been gone far too long that evening, and he wanted to know why.

She and the nice human from the manor strolled ahead of him, stopping now and then to look at garden features.

"My brothers and I used to play in that fountain," he said. "We'd line our cars and trucks up on the rim and send them through the car wash."

His person laughed, the light, tinkling sound that meant she was happy. "It must have been wonderful growing up here. Castleton is full of great places to play."

"It still is," he said. "Race you to the gazebo."

"But I'm wearing—hold on. I'll take them off." She slipped off her shoes and held them in one hand.

Then the pair raced down the allée, feet flying on the thick, soft grass.

It was a tie. Of course the cat beat them using a shortcut. He was faster in general and would have won on the grass too. But he hadn't wanted to spoil their fun.

"The stars are magnificent from this spot," his person said.

"I used to put up my little telescope right here on the steps," he said.

The cat smelled something out of place. An intruder—and not a friendly one, he could tell by the twitch of his sensitive nose. He crouched low to the ground and crawled forward.

A dark figure stood in the bushes, watching his owner and the nice human.

Deciding to test that person's intentions, the cat continued forward, oh so silently, and swiped a claw—or five—at a bare leg.

A quickly suppressed yelp and a hasty retreat told the cat all he needed to know.

Now his person was safe.

The next morning, daybreak came far too soon for Faith's liking. After dinner, a number of people had sat around listening to music and chatting, including Brooke, Luis, Taylor, and Wolfe. Then, around midnight, Wolfe had walked her home through the soft summer night, stars freckling the inky sky above. It had been a great ending to a wonderful evening.

Faith reached out to stroke the cat curled up next to her in bed. "I'm sure he regards me as nothing more than a work acquaintance."

Watson purred, blinking in delight. "I think you're pretty special," his expression seemed to say, "especially when you rub my chin."

"That's because I feed you on a regular basis," Faith said.

The cat opened his eyes wide, appearing wounded by her comment.

"I'm sorry. I know you love me." Faith gave him a final ear rub before throwing off the covers and rolling out of bed. "I love you too."

After showering, Faith put on the outfit Charlotte had provided for the day—a cream linen dress worn with short gloves and topped with a gaudy cloche hat. Faith regarded herself in the mirror with amusement. "Except for the flowerpot on my head, not too bad."

When Faith arrived at the manor, she found several limos pulled up in front. One of the drivers checked a clipboard and directed her to the limo in the middle. Inside, she joined Lorraine, Brooke, and Taylor, all wearing similar outfits to hers.

"Ready for a day at the races?" Lorraine asked Faith.

Faith nodded and settled in the seat beside Brooke. "You got the day off? That's great."

"Sure did." Brooke smiled at Faith. "Love that hat."

Faith regarded Brooke's hat with its tuft of green and blue feathers. "I love yours too." She turned to Lorraine. "Where's Oren?"

"He's racing today so he went ahead with the Jaxons. Wolfe is racing too. One of the other drivers dropped out."

Taylor, who had been busy texting, set her phone in her lap with a sigh. "Almost got my first client. I'm this close." She held up her forefinger and thumb an inch apart.

"Congrats," Brooke said, echoed by the others.

Someone rapped on the tinted window next to Taylor.

Taylor rolled down the glass to reveal Luis, handsome in a lightweight summer suit. "Hi, honey. I thought you had already left for the track."

Luis thrust out his lower lip. "No, I'm afraid there's been a change of plans. The police want to question me."

Taylor flung herself back against the soft leather seat in dismay. "What? Why would they do that? You already talked to them."

His expression was rueful. "Remember how I was practicing my driving when Avis was hit by a ball? They think I might have been responsible."

"How can that be?" Taylor's brow creased.

"Someone saw me teeing off near the clubhouse. I was shooting the other way, but all I had to do is turn around and the ball could have conceivably reached the porch." He bent and gave her a quick kiss. "Don't worry. Everything will be fine."

"Call me, okay?" Taylor said. "Will we see you later?"

Luis checked his watch. "I should be able to get up there by lunchtime. Save me a seat." He gave the car at large a wave and a smile. "Ladies."

"That man is so handsome," Lorraine said after he walked away and Taylor rolled up the window.

The driver slid behind the wheel and started the engine. As the vehicle began to move, soothing classical strains filled the cabin.

Brooke nudged Faith with her elbow. Under the cover of the music, she whispered, "And a murder suspect." Her blue eyes were filled with concern as she studied her cousin, now texting again.

Why did the police suspect Luis? He seemed to have the least motive. Then Faith remembered a connection between Lorraine and Luis. "Lorraine, you said you used to be Luis's teacher?" She kept her tone light, as if making conversation.

At her fiancé's name, Taylor stopped her incessant texting and lifted her head to listen.

Lorraine's gaze was reminiscent. "I was indeed. He was one of my best students." She laughed. "Oh, I know it's easy to say that in hindsight, after a student becomes famous. But he was gifted in writing and storytelling from a young age. We take them at age four there, you know."

"Did I hear his mother worked there too?" Faith asked.

Lorraine frowned and fidgeted with the hem of her dress. "Yes, Carmen worked there for many years." She started to say more but shut her mouth firmly.

"What happened?" Taylor asked. "Luis has hinted around about it, but I have no idea what the whole story is." She winced. "I suppose I'm being nosy."

Lorraine's cheeks colored. "It's not exactly a secret, although it's not pleasant to talk about. Avis basically hounded Carmen out of her teaching position. She hasn't taught school since. In fact, her health is very poor. It's a good thing Luis can afford to support her."

"He's a wonderful man," Taylor said. Her eyes flashed. "No matter what the police think."

The racetrack was near a coastal town just over the New Hampshire border. Faith peered out the window curiously as they trundled up a wide drive lined with light poles, landscaped grounds extending beyond. Ahead was a parking lot circling the stadium containing the oval track.

The limos stopped at the VIP entrance at one side, forming a line.

"Looks like we're getting special treatment," Brooke remarked.

"The Jaxons are first-class all the way," Lorraine said. "They're a wonderful family."

The driver held the door open for them, as did an attendant at the VIP entrance. Their names were checked off a list, and they entered an elevator, which whisked them upstairs to a private box. This held rows of seats, a food service area, and private bathrooms. The ladies sat in front of the picture windows.

Down on the track, vintage race cars were lined up. Faith spotted Wolfe talking to his brother Blake and his mother. Wolfe held a helmet under his arm, which meant he did plan on racing. Oren strolled up to them.

"I think I'll go down and say hello to my sweetie," Lorraine said. "I'll be right back." She headed toward the elevator.

A server in a white shirt and bow tie approached. "What can I get you ladies?"

They ordered coffee and tea. When he returned with the hot beverages, he passed around lunch menus. "I'll be back later to take your selections."

Brooke, seated beside Faith, elbowed her. "Crabmeat salad on croissants. Steak au jus. Grilled salmon. My, they're certainly treating us right."

"I'll say." Faith turned to Taylor, sitting on her other side. "What are you having?" To her surprise, the young woman was sitting slumped, one hand over her eyes. "What's the matter? Are you ill?"

Taylor shook her head, not looking at Faith. "I'm worried." Her voice was a monotone.

"About Luis?" Faith guessed. She felt sympathy for Taylor's plight—having her fiancé suspected of murder. Or at least a person of interest. "You know Chief Garris is extremely fair. Maybe he thinks Luis saw something important."

"I doubt it. Someone ratted him out, remember?" Tears glinted in her eyes.

Brooke left her chair and came to crouch beside Taylor. "Have a little faith. It will be all right." But the expression she cast toward Faith revealed she had her own fears.

Taylor reached for a napkin and wiped her eyes. "All right. I'll try." Her phone dinged and she grabbed it. "Oh, just got a message from an author." She leaped out of her seat. "I need to call him."

"Good idea. Keep your mind off things." Brooke returned to her seat and picked up her coffee cup.

Out on the tarmac, the cars moved into position.

The loudspeaker crackled. "Ladies and gentlemen, the drivers are preparing for our first race. Wolfe Jaxon is behind the wheel of a racing Model T that belonged to his great-grandfather."

As the announcer droned on, Faith watched Wolfe get into what was a pretty dull-looking car compared to the colorful Bentleys, Bearcats, and Bugattis rolling into position.

"This is exciting," Brooke said. "I didn't think I'd like it, but it's fun."

Faith agreed. "Vintage cars are certainly more interesting to look at than modern ones, at least in my eyes."

The race itself was full of ups and downs and hairpin turns. Wolfe was in the lead for a good part of it, but he suffered an engine failure and went sputtering to the side of the track.

Faith and Brooke both groaned in disappointment, joined by the crowd in the booth and outside.

Oren, behind the wheel of a sleek black Rolls-Royce, roared to the finish as the winner. Lorraine, who'd remained down on the track, took the winner's bouquet away from the young woman presenting and gave it to her husband with a big kiss.

"It appears she's forgiven him," Faith said. She filled Brooke in on the scene the night before, how Oren's book was sadly more appealing because of Avis's demise.

"Interesting." Brooke thought for a moment. "The problem with this case is that too many people had reasons to resent Avis." After glancing around the room at the other spectators, she lowered her voice. "Luis, Eban, Oren, and Taylor. And probably a couple more we don't even know about."

"Then there's the confusion about the golf ball incident," Faith commented. "Was it murder or an accident?"

Taylor, who'd been sitting in a corner talking on her phone, came striding back to join them. "Time for lunch yet? I'm starving." She grinned. "Luis is on his way. And he hasn't been charged with anything. What a relief."

"It must be," Brooke said. "As for lunch, I'm having the crabmeat."

"Me too," Faith echoed.

A flurry at the door announced the arrival of Wolfe, Blake, and Charlotte, with others in the Castleton party following. Charlotte and Hildegarde were dressed in jumpsuits, prepared for the powder-puff race to be held right after the meal.

Lunch was served at tables in the room, and Faith was seated between Wolfe and Charlotte.

"I'm sorry your car broke down," Faith said. "It must have been such a disappointment."

Wolfe sliced into his steak with a shrug. "I had a feeling that might happen. But I gave it my best shot. It was still nice taking the old beast for a drive."

"Your father used to take it out too," Charlotte chimed in. "Once it backfired horribly right in downtown Lighthouse Bay, and several people flung themselves to the ground thinking it was gunfire."

Everyone laughed, then began to trade amusing stories about vehicles.

"Would you like a tour of the pit?" Wolfe asked Faith. "We'll have time before the powder-puff race starts." He grinned. "You'll get an inside look at the inner workings of the racetrack."

"Sure. That sounds interesting."

Brooke gave her a significant look that said, "You go, girl."

In the end, a group went down to the track, including Luis, who'd arrived halfway through lunch. The cars taking part in the second race were in the pit being serviced for the event.

Among the mechanics was Eban, dressed in a blue jumpsuit like the other crew. He waved. "This is more fun than tinkering with lawn mowers," he called to Faith and Wolfe.

"I'll bet," Faith called back. "So this is where the phrase *pit stop* came from." She eyed the line of vehicles.

Wolfe laughed. "I suppose so. The cars pull in here during the race for fuel and repairs." He patted his pocket, then pulled out the car key Watson had found. "That reminds me. I never did ask Eban about this. It flew clean out of my mind that day at the country club when Avis—" He shook his head.

"You've been carrying that around with you the whole time?" Faith asked as they walked over to Eban.

"Yes, believe it or not." When they reached the young Castleton employee, Wolfe spent a couple of minutes admiring the car he was prepping. Then he held up the key. "We found this in the manor's herb garden a couple of days ago. Is it yours by chance?"

Eban took the key and studied it. A strange expression flitted over his face. "It's the same make and model as my car all right." His brow furrowed. "If it is mine, how did it get onto Castleton's grounds?"

"That's a good question," Wolfe said. He took the key back and put it carefully into his pocket. "I'll pass it along to the police. Maybe they can figure it out."

As they walked away, Faith sensed Eban staring after them. Did the key exonerate or implicate him? This case was so puzzling.

"Come see the car Mother is driving." Seeming to put the mystery of the key out of his mind, Wolfe led the way to a low-slung Bentley convertible with shiny cream paint.

Charlotte had the hood up and was checking around underneath. "What do you think of my baby?" she asked.

"It's gorgeous," Faith said. Indeed, the automobile was pristine and polished, paint and chrome gleaming in the sun. Even the tires were spotless.

"Thank you." Charlotte studied the car. "I think so too." She pointed at the green Aston Martin beside them. "But that's the car to beat."

Hildegarde stood up from behind the Aston Martin, where she'd been adjusting something, her mechanic at her side.

"Is Hildegarde a skilled driver?" Faith asked.

Wolfe laughed. "I sure hope so. Otherwise that car will be driving *her*."

Hildegarde must have sensed them talking about her, for she looked over and waved with a big smile. "Isn't she a beauty?" she called. "I'm going to smoke you, Mrs. Charlotte Jaxon."

Charlotte struck a sassy pose. "Not likely, Mrs. Maxwell."

Wolfe and Faith continued walking along the pit area, stopping to admire each vehicle. Faith wasn't really into automobiles, but she respected the designs of a past era when distinctive craftsmanship was the order of the day.

"Most modern cars are boring by comparison," she said while gazing at a red Duesenberg loaded with chrome. "They all look the same."

"I agree with you there," Wolfe said. He stopped walking. "Faith, please be careful. Until the police figure out who killed Avis, I want you to stay out of harm's way."

Surprised laughter bubbled up in Faith's chest. She was both flattered and touched that he was concerned for her safety. "I appreciate you saying that, but why would I be in danger?"

"They're taking far too long to figure this out for my liking. And you have a . . . knack, shall we say, for solving mysteries. Don't do anything foolish."

"I promise I won't. And if I feel tempted to, I'll tell you so you can stop me. How's that?"

"Perfect."

A bugle blew, announcing the next race.

"Let's get out of the way. Mother's race is about to begin."

The cars pulled out of the service bays and moved to the starting line. By the time Wolfe and Faith reached the private box, the race was under way.

The glossy automobiles sped around the track with a thrilling thunder of racing engines and jockeyed for position. Charlotte was an excellent driver, maneuvering through slight openings that made Faith wince.

Then Hildegarde swerved, almost hitting the other cars.

It was obvious she'd lost control of the Aston Martin.

15

The spectators in the private box gasped, pressing closer to the glass. Faith held her breath and prayed.

The announcer squawked in alarm, and rescue personnel bolted from their stations, ready to help when the car stopped.

With a final lurch, Hildegarde narrowly missed hitting a concrete retaining wall and rattled to a halt on a strip of grass near the private box.

Emergency vehicles fired up and raced to the spot.

Hildegarde emerged from the car, raising her hands in a victory shake. The crowd roared in approval and relief. Then she collapsed on the grass, arousing an equal volume of concerned exclamations.

The other race cars also screeched to a halt, parking every which way on the course, and drivers sprinted over to the scene.

Without thinking, Faith dashed for the exit, concerned for the older woman. Had something happened to her car? Had she fallen ill? These thoughts churned through Faith's mind as she scurried down the stairs.

"Keep your distance," the track EMT ordered as Faith joined the crowd circling Hildegarde.

The onlookers stepped back only slightly, still craning their necks to see what was going on.

Another EMT was hunkered down and examining Hildegarde, who appeared fine but shaken.

"What happened?" Faith asked the nearest person, a middle-aged man standing with a group of friends.

"One of the wheels was wobbling. It's lucky she wasn't killed." He pointed to the concrete wall. "She almost hit that head-on."

The car had left deep, swerving divots in the grass where Hildegarde had traveled, attempting to stop.

Hildegarde lifted her head. "Someone tried to kill me. The damage to my car was deliberate. It was fine when I inspected it." Her voice was loud enough for even those on the fringe to hear.

Murmurs of outrage rippled through the crowd.

Shock lanced through Faith. *Someone tried to kill Hildegarde? But why? Does she know something about Avis's death?*

"Easy." Wolfe took Faith's elbow, preventing her from falling over. "Did she just say that someone sabotaged the Aston Martin?"

Faith looked at Wolfe, grateful for his strong, calm presence. "Yes, she did. Do you think it's true?"

She read the answer in his eyes. Wolfe shared her suspicions about the connection to Avis. He put both hands on her shoulders to steady her further and said, "Let's go find out."

Glad to be included, Faith followed as Wolfe pushed through the tightly packed bodies. Upon seeing that he was a Jaxon, they made way for the pair. Blake had also arrived and was standing with Charlotte and the track manager. A mechanic examined the front wheel on the driver's side while they all watched.

The mechanic gestured for Blake and the manager to come over. "Take a look at this." He twisted the lug nuts on the wheel. Each one spun easily. "They're all loose." He jerked the tire back and forth. "See? The whole wheel almost fell off."

"Get the pit mechanic," Blake ordered. "He should have caught that." He turned to the manager. "Please get everyone back to their seats. We'll restart the race in a few minutes. In the meantime, have the band play a few songs."

The band for the after-party was already set up on a stage at one end of the stadium.

The throng gradually dispersed at the urging of the track manager and other staff, but Faith lingered, wanting to stay with Wolfe. Charlotte and the rest of the drivers jumped into their cars and roared off around the track to the starting line.

Cleared by the EMTs, Hildegarde was leaning against her car, sipping a bottle of water.

Spotting an opportunity to speak to her, Faith leaned against the car beside her, careful not to scratch the glossy paint. "I'm so glad you're okay." On the stage, the band began playing a lively rock tune, and Faith had to raise her voice to be heard. "That was really scary to watch. I can't imagine actually driving a car in a situation like that."

Hildegarde chuckled. "Tell me about it. It was all I could do not to hit anyone else." She traced the Aston Martin's lines with a finger. "But she's a good old gal. I was able to bring her to a stop without flipping over or crashing."

"Thank goodness you're such a great driver."

"I have lots of experience," Hildegarde said. "I've won quite a few powder-puff races." She motioned toward the track. "Here comes Billy. He was my prerace mechanic."

The slender and wiry mechanic jogged along the edge of the track from the service area, a confused and scared expression on his freckled face. "I'm sorry, Mrs. Maxwell. I would have been here sooner, but I was taking my lunch. Joe was supposed to watch your bay in case you needed something."

"And so he did." Hildegarde pointed to one of the men working on the Aston Martin. "But the problem happened on the track. My wheel was loose."

Billy's mouth dropped open. "Loose? But how can that be?" He pulled off his cap and ran his fingers through cropped red hair, casting bewildered and worried glances at the Aston Martin.

Blake and Wolfe joined them.

"Billy, did you check the wheels before Mrs. Maxwell got in the car?" Blake asked. His tone was stern but calm, and he didn't sound accusatory.

Billy put his cap back on and straightened it. "Of course I did. I used the prerace checklist, like always." He screwed up his face. "I've been working for you for three years, Mr. Jaxon, and nothing like this has ever happened on my watch."

"I know that." Blake studied the Aston Martin. "Were you with the car every minute before the race?"

Billy hesitated. "No sir. I stepped away for a minute to use the restroom. Joe took over for me."

Blake turned to study the other mechanic, who was checking the lug nuts one more time. "I'll speak to Joe about that." He swung back around. "Mrs. Maxwell, did you leave the service bay at any time?"

Hildegarde gave a little laugh. "I'm afraid so. I always make a pit stop of my own before a race."

Faith pictured the chaotic scene she'd witnessed in the pit, with guests, drivers, and crew milling about the area. If Hildegarde and Billy had stepped away at the same time, someone must have taken advantage of the opportunity to tamper with the lug nuts. Joe, busy with another vehicle, probably didn't notice.

Blake rubbed his chin, considering the situation. "I'll check the cameras, but I don't think they fully cover that area."

"You need to call the police," Hildegarde said. "Someone tried to kill me. If I wasn't such a good driver . . ." Hands over her face, she shuddered, shoulders sagging.

Wolfe hastily stepped to the woman's side and propped her up. "Let's get you inside. Shock must be setting in."

Joe finished with the wheel and asked Blake, "What do you want me to do next?"

"Drive it back to the bay," Blake said. "And have the guys check all the cars before we start the race again. I don't want another incident."

Instead of returning to the private box, the small group went to Blake's suite of offices overlooking the course. Hildegarde was settled comfortably on a sofa in the waiting area. No one had asked Faith to leave so she sat beside Hildegarde to offer support.

"Would you ladies like refreshments?" Blake asked. "I can have some cold drinks sent up."

"That sounds nice. Thank you," Faith said.

Hildegarde didn't answer. The older woman huddled in a corner of the sofa, staring at her interlaced fingers.

Wolfe glanced at Hildegarde, then sent Faith a concerned look. "Keep an eye on things for us, okay? I'm going to give Chief Garris a call while Blake contacts the local force."

"I'll do that," Faith said. As he and his brother disappeared into Blake's adjacent office, Faith dug her phone out of her bag and sent Brooke a text. The others must be wondering what had happened to her and what was going on with Hildegarde.

Brooke responded immediately, her answer decorated with exclamation points. *Keep me posted*, she concluded.

I will, Faith wrote back.

With a knock on the door, a staff person entered, wheeling a cart holding ice buckets filled with soft drinks, bottled water, and juices.

Faith thanked him, then rose from her seat to make a selection. "What would you like, Hildegarde?"

Hildegarde made a half-hearted gesture. "Whatever."

Faith dug two bottles of strawberry kiwi juice out of the ice and brought them over. She opened both and handed Hildegarde one. "This looks refreshing." She hoped the sugary drink would stave off the shock and help the other woman perk up.

"Thanks," Hildegarde said. She drank the bottle in several long swallows. "I guess I was thirstier than I thought." To Faith's relief, color began to return to her face.

Through the half-open door to Blake's office, Faith heard the brothers talking, their voices a low rumble. No doubt the police would soon arrive and she would lose her opportunity to talk to the widow. With a sense of urgency, she asked, "Do you really think someone tampered with your wheel?"

Hildegarde frowned. "I didn't imagine it. Lug nuts don't loosen themselves. When Billy checked them earlier, they were fine." Her tone was astringent.

"Of course they don't," Faith agreed hastily. "But I can't understand why a nice woman like you would be targeted for malicious mischief."

"I do." Hildegarde regarded Faith steadily with cold blue eyes. "I've been talking to the police about Avis's death. And someone obviously doesn't like that."

Before Faith could respond, the door to the office rattled open, and Charlotte, dressed in her racing jumpsuit, burst in. "Hildegarde, how are you?" She bent and gave her friend a hug. Resting her hands on Hildegarde's shoulders, she leaned back and said, "I've never seen such masterful driving in my life. You could handle the Indy 500."

The jesting had the desired effect, for Hildegarde smiled slyly in return. "See, I told you I was good. I would have beaten you." She shivered. "But not today."

Charlotte plopped down on the sofa. "Just say the word, and I'll cancel the whole thing." She gestured toward the scene outside the wide windows. "It feels wrong somehow, having the festivities continue while this . . . *situation* is going on."

Hildegarde reached for Charlotte's hand. "No, you mustn't cancel. You've put far too much work into this event. And aren't the proceeds going to the children's hospital? You can't disappoint the little tykes. So please, go get in your car and show them all how it's done."

"All right, if you're sure." Charlotte peered out the window. "I'd better scoot. They're about ready to blow the bugle." She turned to Faith. "Thanks for being so supportive. Once we get through today, we need to discuss tomorrow's pet show at the country club."

"I'll be around when you need me," Faith promised.

The pet show was a last-minute brainstorm of Charlotte's, featuring a parade of dogs, cats, and other animals around the putting green, inspired by a similar event in the 1920s. Faith planned to bring

Watson, even though he disdained such events. She wasn't sure if he objected to the examination by judges or being attached to a leash. She suspected both.

Charlotte poked her head into the inner sanctum to say hello to her sons. Then, as quickly as she had arrived, she was gone again.

Faith wandered to the window to watch the race cars roll into position. From this vantage point, she saw Charlotte jump into her Bentley convertible and roar onto the track. The band stopped playing, and the announcer started talking again, sound that was piped into these rooms too.

Faith realized she was still thirsty. "Would you like something else to drink?" she asked her companion.

Hildegarde sank into a chair with a better view of the proceedings. "Yes, please. How about water this time?"

While Faith was sorting through the ice bucket, there was a knock on the door.

Before she could answer, Blake emerged from the office. "That's the police." He opened the door to reveal two men, one of whom was Chief Garris, dressed in a polo shirt, shorts, and deck shoes.

"Good morning, Chief." Faith paused in the act of plucking a bottle of water from the melting ice. "You got here quickly." She wiped off the droplets with a napkin and reached for another.

"I was visiting family nearby so I was able to get here in a jiffy." Garris scanned the room, nodding at Wolfe, who stood in the office doorway, and Hildegarde, seated near the window. "Somebody want to tell me what happened and why you think it relates to my case?"

Wolfe filled him in, and then Garris and local officer Ben Carter interviewed Hildegarde.

After Hildegarde returned to the private box, Faith, Wolfe, Chief Garris, and Officer Carter convened in Blake's office to study the security footage from the pit. Wolfe insisted Faith join them because he said she was a great observer.

Blake flicked through the screens, bringing up the camera closest to the bay where the Aston Martin had been parked.

There was a simultaneous groan of disappointment. Only part of the Aston Martin was in view—the rear half.

"What is that blocking the camera?" Wolfe pointed at the tall, boxy item hiding the front end of the car.

His brother made a noise of disgust. "It looks like one of our tall toolboxes. Isn't that convenient?"

It certainly is—for the vandal. Faith wondered if the person had moved the tools to block the camera or if it was merely a coincidence.

Standing with arms crossed, Garris asked, "Do you have a window of time when someone could have tampered with the car? I assume it's checked over before the race."

"We have a step-by-step procedure in place as part of our safety plan," Blake said. "I've asked Billy to bring up the log to find out when he looked at the wheels." The outer door opened and shut. "That's probably him now."

With a knock on the inner doorway, Billy poked his head in. "I've got the log." At Blake's gesture, he entered and handed the clipboard to Wolfe, who was closest.

Wolfe scanned the checklist, then showed it to Blake, running his finger along the entries. "Look at this. There's more than an hour between when he checked them and when the race started."

Blake gave a low whistle as he worked the keyboard, rewinding the video to the correct time. "That's the time slot we'll look at. Thanks, Billy." He pointed to the screen. "Oh, and it's a little late now, but can you please move that toolbox?"

Billy stared at the object with chagrin. "I'm sorry. I don't know who put that there. I'll take care of it right away." With slumped shoulders, he scurried out of the room.

"Poor guy," Wolfe said. "He obviously feels responsible."

"He's a good worker and reliable. I won't hold this incident against him, especially since I have no doubt he did his job correctly and someone else loosened that wheel." Blake pushed a button on the keyboard. "All right, let's take a look."

Faith stared at the screen, barely blinking in case she missed something vital. But the only thing she saw was the bustle of workers moving about the space, joined by drivers and guests. All of Charlotte's friends visited the car at one time or another, lingering to admire its lines.

Blake stopped the footage when the Aston Martin drove off to the starting line.

Chief Garris grunted. "I didn't see anything conclusive, but on the other hand, nothing is ruled out either."

"What do you mean?" Blake swiveled around to face the chief, arms folded across his chest. "Do you think we can figure out who sabotaged the car?"

"Not from that video," Garris said. "But it's another piece of the puzzle. We'll be making an arrest soon."

16

Who will you be arresting? Faith wanted to ask Chief Garris. She could tell by the expressions on Blake's and Wolfe's faces that they shared her curiosity.

The room was quiet for a long, tense moment before Wolfe broke the silence. "I sincerely hope you do make an arrest soon and bring Avis's killer to justice. Let us know if we can do anything to help."

Garris acknowledged the offer with a nod as he slid back his chair and stood. "That's it for now. Thanks for your cooperation." To Officer Carter, he said, "I'll go down to the station with you so we can compare notes."

"That would be great. I want to get to the bottom of this." Officer Carter turned to Blake. "I'll need to take that recording into custody."

"Of course." Blake saved the files onto a thumb drive and handed it to Officer Carter, who slipped it into an evidence envelope. Blake shook hands with Garris, then Carter. "I appreciate you both coming by. And if I learn anything new on this end, I'll call immediately."

"Please do, Mr. Jaxon," Officer Carter said. "We value your business in this town, and we want to nip any incidents like this in the bud. Perhaps we can station a patrol officer here for the next couple of races, just in case."

"That's a very generous offer," Blake said, ushering them toward the door. "If we don't find the culprit before the next race day, I'll take you up on it."

Once Garris and Carter were gone, Wolfe said fervently, "I'm so sorry about this, Blake. I hoped we were doing you a good turn by having the event here, not bringing trouble to your doorstep."

"It's not your fault. And look at this." Blake clicked to a social media site, where videos of Hildegarde's careening journey around the track had been posted. He shared a rueful smile. "As they say, there's no such thing as bad publicity. Let's hope this mess translates into ticket sales."

During the remainder of the racetrack event, which stretched well into the evening, Faith puzzled over the sabotage and Chief Garris's claim that he was close to an arrest. Were the two related, or had Hildegarde merely been seeking attention after an unfortunate accident? She certainly seemed to bask in the limelight accorded her as a heroine, which eclipsed even Charlotte's win of the powder-puff race. If Hildegarde had been targeted by the killer, why? What did she know that put her in danger?

These circular thoughts diminished Faith's enjoyment of the trackside pulled pork barbecue accompanied by music that ranged from jazz to country to rock and roll. But the hundreds of other people at the event appeared to be having a good time.

Brooke joined Faith, who was standing by herself watching a group of guests attempt line dancing. "I wanted to let you know the car is leaving soon." She yawned. "I can't wait to get home. I've got the breakfast shift tomorrow."

"And I've got the pet show." Faith scanned the crowd for Charlotte and spotted her sitting with a group of friends. "Charlotte and I haven't had a chance to go over the final arrangements yet."

Brooke leaned close and whispered, "I love Charlotte, but won't you be a wee bit glad when things get back to normal?"

Faith laughed. "I have to admit I will. The idea of working in the library sounds positively heavenly right about now."

The sous-chef wiggled her fingers. "And give me some new recipes to experiment with, please. That's my happy place."

"And we're definitely grateful for that." Faith linked arms with her friend. "Let's go corral Charlotte."

Charlotte wasn't ready to leave, so she promised Faith they'd meet in the morning at breakfast. "Almost everything is ready," she assured Faith. "It won't be too bad."

Faith wasn't quite as confident, but she smiled and said, "See you then. Have a good night." As she and Brooke walked away, she asked, "Can you please make French toast for me tomorrow morning? I can tell I'm going to need a treat."

"Sure thing. With real maple syrup."

Brooke and Faith were alone in the limo for the ride home, and they dozed off as the big car sailed through quiet towns and along winding roads back to the manor. Both were slightly groggy when they climbed out and thanked the driver.

"Do you want to sleep over at my place tonight?" Faith asked. She knew Brooke kept spare work clothing in her locker at the manor. "I have extra toiletries and pajamas."

"That sounds good. Especially since I have to be here so early. Taylor can feed Diva and Bling for me. They'll miss me, but it's just one night." Brooke's pet angelfish were surprisingly interactive according to their owner.

They fell into step, crunching along the path to Faith's cottage.

"What a beautiful night," Faith said. The warm air was like silk against her skin, and the stars were dazzling diamonds in a field of black velvet.

"It sure is. I love summer evenings." Brooke took a deep breath and flung her arms out. "We have to store up the memories for the winter. Winter lasts so long on the Cape."

"I know," Faith replied. "Sometimes it seems like it will never end."

As they approached the cottage, Faith spotted a huddled

shape on the steps. With a little shriek, she grabbed Brooke's arm. "What's that?"

Brooke stopped dead, craning her neck. "I don't know. A person sitting there?"

The shape uncoiled from the step and stood. "Faith?" a woman asked in trembling tones. "I'm so glad you're home."

Faith recognized the voice and hurried forward. "Kate, are you all right?"

The answer was a sob.

Dread shot through Faith, and she moved even faster to her friend's side. Putting an arm around Kate, she asked, "What's the matter? Is it your mom? Or your dad?" She held her breath, waiting for the answer.

"No." Kate gave a tiny laugh. "Nothing that horrible. But I got fired!"

"Fired? What for?" Brooke stood with hands on hips, ready to go into battle.

"They found that lost necklace in my locker. The one I told you about at the fashion show, Faith." Kate wiped her eyes. "The manager said they might press charges."

"Just because it was in your locker doesn't mean you stole it," Brooke said stoutly. "Why did they look in your locker anyway?"

Faith also wanted to know the answer to that, but she thought this discussion was better continued in the cottage. "Come inside. I think this situation calls for chocolate." She unlocked the door and stood back to let them enter.

Watson greeted them, giving Faith a sullen mew.

"I'm sorry. I know I've been neglecting you." Faith bent to pet her cat. "Let's get a snack."

He knew the meaning of that word and darted ahead of the three women, leading the way.

In the kitchen, Faith filled his dish and gave him fresh water.

In the meantime, Brooke dug through the freezer and found a

container of chocolate ice cream. She scooped some into three bowls and added a few sliced strawberries and whipped cream as garnish.

Kate stared at the bowl Brooke handed her. "Wow. This looks awesome."

"That's what I like to hear." Brooke winked. "The strawberries make it healthy, by the way."

"Keep telling yourself that," Faith said wryly.

Faith wasn't a bit hungry, but she took a spoonful anyway. After allowing Kate to take a few bites, she said, "All right, take it from the top. What happened?"

Kate set her spoon down. "Remember how I told you that things have gone missing all summer? Some of them you could chalk up to people being careless, right? But my earrings, for one, were in my purse, so they were definitely stolen."

"Did the manager ever do anything about that?" Brooke interjected.

"We reported it to the police. But nothing else as far as figuring out who is taking stuff." Kate paused. "Until tonight. Someone gave him an anonymous tip that the necklace was in one of the lockers. He searched them all, and it was in mine."

"You didn't notice it earlier?" Brooke asked.

Kate shook her head. "It was tucked in the back, in the crack where the wall and floor meet. They used a flashlight to find it. I never would have noticed it."

Definitely planted by someone clever. "What kind of locks do they use on the lockers?" Faith asked.

"Just regular padlocks. They issue them to staff." Kate picked up her spoon and took another bite. She seemed to be feeling a little better, judging by her demeanor. "The guests bring their own."

"I wonder if padlocks are easy to pick." Brooke grabbed her smartphone and tapped away.

"Brooke!" Kate's mouth dropped open. "What are you planning to do?"

"That's a reasonable question considering Brooke's track record," Faith teased. "But I think she's just trying to figure out how someone got into your locker."

"Aha! You *can* pick regular padlocks. Apparently it's not that hard." Brooke pursed her lips. "Who knew?"

Faith's pulse gave a leap of excitement. "That must be the answer. Someone broke into your locker and stole your earrings, and now they're trying to pin the thefts on you."

Kate groaned. "Lucky me." Her shoulders slumped. "What am I going to do? If this gets out, it could affect the rest of my life. Even jeopardize my scholarship."

"The first thing to do is tell your parents. They need to speak to Marvin Treadwell on your behalf. And in my opinion, the fact someone broke into your locker once before is reason enough to cast doubt on your guilt." Faith was energized by a charge of righteous zeal. "I'm going to be at the country club tomorrow, and I'll talk to the manager too. Don't worry. We'll figure it out."

"You think so?" Kate's face brightened with hope. "I'm so glad I came over here. I couldn't quite face Mom yet, and I knew you would give me good advice." She got up from the table and gave Faith and Brooke big hugs.

Faith squeezed Kate in return, hoping and praying that she would be able to help Midge's daughter.

"Hold still, Rumpy. I'm almost finished." Faith ran the soft brush over Watson's fur one last time. Then she fastened a fancy new collar around his neck. He usually wore plain ones, but Faith had spotted this white collar decorated with curly black mustaches in Castleton Manor's pet spa. It was perfect with Watson's tuxedo cat coloring.

"All done." She gave him a pat.

He stared at her, blinking.

Faith laughed. "I know. But a deal's a deal." She'd promised him his favorite treat from Midge's pet bakery if he behaved while being groomed.

As Watson crunched the tunaroon, Faith remembered her promise to Kate the night before. When she got to the country club, she'd visit the manager first. He needed to realize that Kate had friends in the community who would vouch for her character.

At the club, Marvin Treadwell wasn't quite as receptive as she'd hoped. Faith stood inside the doorway to his office, where he sat shuffling papers behind his desk. Next to her sat Watson, looking regal and ready for the pet show. His leash rested in her purse, ready for use during the actual show.

"I'm sorry, Miss Newberry," he said in his squeaky voice. "I really can't discuss an employee issue with you."

"I get that, but Kate isn't guilty." Faith heard her voice rising in volume and tried to tamp it down. "This false accusation could ruin her life."

Marvin stopped moving the papers and stared at her. "It's not that I'm unsympathetic. We're not moving ahead with charges at this time because there's no proof Miss Foster took the item in question. We only found it in her locker. I don't like anonymous tips any more than you do."

Relief coursed through Faith, and she had to grip the doorjamb for a moment to steady herself. "Maybe you should change those locks too. Apparently they're easy to tamper with."

"Yes, thank you," he said tersely. "Sorry to cut this short, but I've got to get back to work."

"Forgive me for interrupting." She glanced down to speak to Watson. He was gone. "Have you seen my cat? He was right here a minute ago."

Marvin peered around the room and under his desk. "He's not in here. Hope you find him."

Me too. Faith ran out into the corridor, where she was rewarded by the sight of Watson's hindquarters vanishing around a corner.

His person needed help. She was better than other humans at just about everything that mattered, but once in a while, she was clueless.

The cat trotted down the corridor, his sensitive nose picking up odors from the carpet. Spilled soda here, a trace of mud there. Cracker crumbs everywhere. What happened—an explosion? Ah, there it was, the scent identifying the prowler in the garden.

Maybe that was the problem. Human noses didn't work right. If they did, they could follow the trail that led to solving this mystery instead of crying and yakking.

A swinging door loomed up ahead, propped open by a yellow bucket. Perfect. Now he wouldn't have to risk bruising his sensitive nose or wait for someone to understand what he wanted. Humans. What was a cat to do?

"Watson, stop. Don't go in there," Faith called.

Her command went unheeded. Watson dashed through an open door clearly marked *Men's Locker Room.*

Faith stopped in the doorway, uncertain what to do. She didn't want to barge in there, where men expected privacy to shower and change. "Watson, get back here."

"What's going on?" Luis, dressed in golf clothing, strode down the hallway. "The ladies' locker room is that way." He pointed in the other direction with a grin.

"I'm so glad to see you. My cat went in there, and he won't come out."

The author's brows rose in amusement. "Is he that handsome black-and-white cat? Hang on. I'll go get him." Whistling, he entered the locker room. "What are you doing, boy? Come on. You don't need to go in there."

What on earth was Watson up to now? Faith was dying to find out. Taking a step inside, she called, "Luis, is anyone else in there?"

"Nope. Just me and the cat. It's all clear if you want to join us." His voice deepened with a note of surprise. "And you might be interested in this."

Looking both ways instinctively, Faith darted inside the locker room. With any luck she'd be in and out in minutes, if not seconds, before an outraged golfer came along.

Luis and Watson were in the second row of lockers. One door hung open, and Watson reached up and batted it as though to demonstrate his role in the matter. Inside the locker was a long, slender, cylindrical object.

"What is that?" Faith asked.

"If I'm not mistaken, that is a homemade gun. Just the right size for shooting golf balls."

17

Faith studied the strange object, allowing Luis's statement to sink in. "You think someone used that to shoot Avis?"

"It makes sense. You know how hard it is to deliberately hit an object with a golf ball? Miss by only a couple of inches and it would have hit Charlotte or Lorraine."

He was right. Faith pictured the three women sitting at the table. Whoever had hit Avis had very bad luck—or very good aim.

Watson, content after showing them his discovery, sat down and began washing.

"Whose locker is it?" Faith asked.

"I have no idea, but let's find out." Luis pulled his phone out of his pocket. "I'm calling the office."

A middle-aged man carrying a duffel bag entered the room and gave them an odd look, especially when he noticed Watson.

Luis waved him away. "Police business. We'll be out of here in a few." Waiting for an answer, he tapped his foot. "Mr. Treadwell's office, please. It's urgent . . . Yes, I'll hold." Finally the manager answered. "Mr. Treadwell, I'm in the men's locker room. There's something in here you need to see. Bring your list of locker assignments."

A couple of minutes later, Marvin rushed into the locker room. "What's she doing in here?" he asked, jerking his thumb at Faith.

"She's with him." Luis pointed at Watson. "And he found something important. See that plastic gun? It's used to shoot golf balls."

Realization didn't take long to sink in, and it rocked the manager back on his heels. "You think it was used . . ." His voice trailed off.

"Exactly. So if I were you, I'd call the police. But first, tell us whose locker this is."

Marvin peered at the number on the door, then consulted his list. "It's assigned to Eban Matthews."

Eban. Tears flooded Faith's eyes, a reaction she wasn't expecting. She genuinely liked the young man and couldn't believe he was the killer, even if the evidence was pointing that way. She clenched her fists. *No, he's innocent. Something's wrong.*

"Hi, guys. What's going on?" Eban appeared around the corner of the lockers. He was dressed in country club attire and appeared totally at ease. The moment that peace fled was visible across his handsome features as quiet happiness gave way to confusion and then to dismay. "What's that thing in my locker?" He bent closer, trying to see the number on the door. "That is my locker, right?"

Marvin tapped his pen on the clipboard. "It is indeed. And we were hoping you could tell us how that thing got in there."

Eban dug in his heels. "I honestly can't. So you tell me."

Faith thought of something. "The locker was open, Luis?"

He nodded.

"Don't you lock it, Eban?"

"I don't bother. I just keep a towel and some soap and shampoo in there. See?" Eban reached for the door, then yanked his hand back at Marvin's admonition.

"No one is to touch anything. I'm calling the police." Marvin headed to a wall phone, then turned and pointed at Eban. "Don't move a muscle."

Eban sagged down onto a bench. "Can I at least sit? I just walked eighteen holes of golf." He slumped against the wall and crossed his arms over his chest.

Luis, from his post leaning against the lockers, watched Eban narrowly.

As for Watson, he sauntered over to the implicated caddy, rubbing against his ankles and purring. Eban reached down and stroked his back. Watson purred even louder.

Faith smiled automatically at the sight of her happy cat—until something puzzling crossed her mind. Watson had led them to what was probably the murder weapon, but he seemed to approve of the person it appeared to belong to.

It didn't add up. Why on earth would Watson do such a thing? Or act that way?

She had plenty of time to ponder that while waiting for the police to arrive. In the meantime, Marvin blocked access to the locker room, sending disgruntled golfers away to the showers in the pool building.

Finally a familiar gruff voice was heard in the hallway, and Chief Garris entered. "So we meet again," he said to Faith. Officer Bryan Laddy was with him.

"Hello, Chief," Faith replied.

Marvin Treadwell appeared dubious at this exchange, but he let it pass without comment, merely bestowing a tight-lipped smile. "Thanks for coming." He led them to Eban's locker. "This is the item in question."

Garris and Laddy exchanged significant glances.

"And how did this come to light?" Garris asked.

Marvin shifted his feet, looking uncomfortable.

Luis spoke up. "The cat found it."

Garris gave a grunt of disbelief. "Say that again?"

Luis winked at Faith. "That must be why you call him Watson."

"He's helped me solve some mysteries," Faith said.

Watson meowed, as though agreeing.

"That's amazing. I knew he was an awesome cat." Eban rubbed Watson's chin just the way he liked it.

"As I said, the cat led me right to it." Luis went through the sequence of events, how Watson had gone into the locker room and he'd offered to retrieve him for Faith. He stated again that the locker was open and the homemade rifle clearly visible.

"And whose locker is this?" Garris asked.

Eban waved a hand. "It's mine. But I never saw that thing before in my life."

"Interesting," Laddy said. "First it was your car that you weren't driving that hit a woman. Now you're telling us you don't own the weapon that killed her, even though it's in your locker."

Eban bolted upright on the bench. "I'm innocent. It's obvious I'm being framed."

Chief Garris put a hand up. "Laddy, take it easy. Let's go slowly."

Laddy's chiseled face reddened. "Sorry, Chief." He eyed the rifle. "I'll take that into custody. Maybe we can get some prints off it."

While Laddy worked on securing the evidence, Chief Garris finished questioning Faith and Luis. As he asked again how Watson had come across the golf ball gun, Faith had to wonder what others who read the police report would think. This had to be the first time in history a feline had discovered evidence in a murder case.

After about ten minutes, they were released and allowed to leave the locker room.

"Are you still going to the pet show?" Luis asked Faith in the hallway. "I was supposed to meet Taylor, but to be honest, I feel kind of discombobulated. What a strange twist of events."

"I have to go," Faith said. "Charlotte is expecting me. But you're right. That whole thing in the locker room was crazy. I refuse to believe Eban is guilty."

"I know. He's a nice guy." Luis rubbed his chin thoughtfully. "But I suppose you never really know people's deepest, darkest secrets." He glanced at his watch. "I've got to make a quick call. If you see Taylor, tell her I'll be along."

As Faith watched the writer stride away, his words rang through her head. *You never really know people's deepest, darkest secrets.*

"Knock, knock." Brooke stood at Faith's back screen door. "You'll have to open up for me. My hands are full."

Faith unlatched the screen and held it open for her friend to enter. "Thanks for bringing dinner."

"My pleasure." Brooke set the containers on the kitchen table. "I've got marinated steak, curried potato salad, and green salad with local ingredients." She held up a mason jar. "And homemade dressing."

Faith popped the potato salad into the fridge. "It sounds fabulous, although I've barely been able to eat all day because I've been so upset." She'd hardly touched the decadent lunch served after the pet show.

"I get that." Brooke pulled plastic wrap off the platter of meat. "I can't believe that whole thing with Watson finding the golf ball gun in Eban's locker."

"Me neither." Faith grabbed a pitcher of iced tea and filled two glasses. "If he is guilty, why would he keep that gun in his locker at the club? You'd think he would have disposed of it somewhere."

"I would have—that's for sure. It's so obvious that he's being framed." Brooke took a sip of tea and put the glass down. "We'll let the meat warm up a bit. Did you start the grill?"

"I will. Let's go out to the patio." Faith picked up a tray of dishes and utensils while Brooke took the two glasses of iced tea. As she placed the tray on the table, the bushes rustled and Watson emerged.

"There's the blue-ribbon cat," Brooke announced, crouching down to pet him. "I love his collar." He was still wearing the mustache-decorated adornment.

"So did the judges. Plus, he was quite the character, as always." Faith smiled, remembering how Watson had charmed the judges with his regal attitude and heart-melting charm. He certainly knew when to purr and when to turn up his nose.

That train of thought reminded Faith of Watson's behavior in the locker room. "You know what was really strange? Watson loves Eban, but he led Luis right to the golf ball gun that implicated him."

Brooke rubbed the cat's chin. "You're just a smarty-pants, aren't you, Watson? I think you were giving us a clue."

Faith turned on the gas grill. "If only I could interpret it."

"We need an expert in kitty language." Brooke stroked Watson's fur, then rose. "Let me go wash up and I'll get cooking."

"Taylor is coming, right?" Faith moved to the table and set out plates, napkins, and silverware.

Brooke paused with the screen door half-open. "She said she was. Luis is busy working with his freelance editor tonight. Guess who it is? Ivy Maxwell."

"Ivy is Luis's editor? I guess that makes sense. Her grandfather was an editor. Maybe that explains why Luis and Ivy hang out a lot together."

"I was worried that Luis was two-timing my cousin," Brooke confessed. "But Taylor told me that's not the case. In fact, it was Taylor's idea for them to work together." She stepped inside, the screen door slapping shut behind her.

Faith was relieved to hear that, but she still wondered if they had something to do with Avis's death. She didn't like the way Luis had been on the spot when the golf ball gun was found. She finished tweaking the place settings. "Come on, Rumpy. Let's get you some dinner."

Inside, Faith fed the cat and refilled the iced tea glasses.

Brooke fished through the drawers for grilling tongs and grabbed shakers of salt and pepper. Then, juggling the meat platter and the other items, she used her hip to open the screen door.

"I love watching you work," Faith joked. "My own private chef."

"Anytime," Brooke said with a laugh. "Come watch my mastery of cooking outdoors over flame."

Someone knocked on the front door.

"There's Taylor now," Faith called as she went to answer it. "We'll be right out."

Despite the heat and humidity, Brooke's cousin looked fresh and pretty in blue linen capris and a white sleeveless top. She flashed a wan smile. "Thanks for inviting me."

Faith wondered what was on Taylor's mind to make her so pensive. "Glad you could make it. We're eating out on the patio." In the kitchen, she took the potato salad out of the fridge and let Taylor carry the tossed salad.

Brooke stood at the grill, tongs in hand, clouds of fragrant smoke streaming from the cooking meat. "How do you want it?"

"I'll take mine medium," Faith said.

"Me too," Taylor said, choosing a seat at the table. "It smells fabulous."

"Iced tea?" Faith asked Taylor.

"That sounds great. Thanks."

Faith nipped back to the kitchen for the pitcher and another glass. She handed Taylor her beverage and sat down. "Ah, it's been a long day."

"I hear you." Taylor's mouth turned down. "I can't believe what's going on with Eban. Luis filled me in."

Earlier when Faith had joined the pet show, she hadn't had time to talk to anyone about the scene she'd witnessed in the locker room. And afterward, Taylor and Luis had slipped away before she could catch up with either of them.

"Is there any more news? I mean, did they actually arrest Eban?" Brooke flipped the meat and checked it. "Another couple of minutes." She left her station and picked up her glass off the table.

"Not that I've heard." Taylor pulled out her phone and flicked through the screens. "No new messages from Eban." She set the phone down. "We've been in touch constantly about his book." Her face crumpled. "How terrible to have this happen to him right now. He's such a good guy."

"Hang in there." Brooke handed her a napkin. "It will be okay."

"I hope so." Taylor wiped her eyes with the napkin. "It's all been too much." She gulped. "So horrible. Poor Avis and now poor Eban."

Brooke returned to the grill. After checking the steak again, she took it off the heat and put it onto a platter. "Eat something. It will make you feel better."

"Yes ma'am," Taylor said, a reluctant smile creasing her lips. "Isn't that what your mother always says?"

"She sure does. I think that's why I decided to become a cook." Brooke sat at the table. "I want to make people feel good." She pushed the bowl of potato salad closer to Taylor. "Try this. It's my own recipe."

For the next few minutes, silence fell as the three friends passed the dishes around.

Faith cut a chunk of thick, juicy steak. It practically melted in her mouth. "Oh, this is heavenly."

Brooke slowly chewed her own bite. "Not bad. I might adjust the marinade."

Faith tried the potato salad next, and the flavors were a tart, savory burst that made her mouth water. "Wow. What's in this?"

"Not the usual. Yogurt, tahini, tiny red chilies, secret spices." Brooke's grin was mischievous. "If I tell you, I'll have to—" She sobered. "Sorry. That was a bad joke."

"It is really good." Taylor scooped up a big forkful. "I never would have guessed those ingredients."

Faith took the opportunity to change the subject. "So tell us about Luis. Have you two set a date yet?"

Taylor laughed. "No, not yet. He needs to meet my parents first. And I'm going to meet his mom when we go back to New York." She shivered. "I'm a little nervous."

"Why?" Brooke asked. "Is she likely to be a monster-in-law?"

"No, I don't think so." Taylor's expression grew thoughtful. "It's just that Luis idolizes his mother so much. I suppose it's foolish, but if she doesn't like me, I'm afraid it might change his feelings for me."

Brooke scoffed. "As if. The guy is gaga over you. Anyone can see that."

Taylor played with her spoon. "You think so?"

"I know so," Brooke said firmly. "And our family is going to love him."

Listening to the cousins, who appeared to be as close as sisters, Faith fervently hoped that Luis wasn't involved in Avis's death. If Eban was innocent, as she hoped he was, then someone else was guilty. *What a feat of logic*, she chided herself. Her thoughts whirled as she considered each person involved in turn . . .

Taylor's phone gave an insistent ring. She casually picked it up to glance at the caller ID. Then she dropped the phone with a clatter. "It's the police," she whispered.

The police? Faith lost her appetite. *This can't be good.*

Taylor's hand quivered as it hovered over the phone. "I'm scared to answer."

"I'll do it." Brooke snatched it up. "Taylor Milner's phone. How can I help you?" She listened. "All right, I'll have her do that." She disconnected and set the phone down. "Chief Garris wants you to call him."

A shaking hand went to Taylor's lips. "Oh no. What is going on?"

"We won't know until you call him," Brooke said. "Come on. Let's get it over with."

Taylor called the station back. She was connected to the chief and listened briefly. "Do I . . ." She cleared her throat and tried again. "Do I need an attorney?"

At those words, Faith's pulse skyrocketed, and by the way Brooke lurched in her chair, it was evident that she was equally alarmed.

"I don't? Good." Taylor sighed deeply after she disconnected. "They want to talk to me. That's all."

"When?" Faith asked.

With another exhale, Taylor pushed back in her chair. "Right now. Will you two go with me?"

Despite the late hour, Daphne Kerrigan was working behind the front desk. The attractive receptionist, with her wavy blonde hair and flawless makeup, usually worked days so she could be home at night with her husband and teenage son.

"Good evening." Daphne looked at the trio curiously. "How may I help you?"

Taylor glanced at Faith and Brooke before blurting, "I'm Taylor Milner. Here to see the chief." Her knees quivered, and Brooke offered a supporting hand.

Daphne picked up the phone. "Have a seat. He'll be right with you."

Faith glanced around the station as they sat down, taking in posters of the FBI's most wanted and the big round clock on the wall. The atmosphere was quiet yet tense. Beyond the safety glass barrier, evidence was being weighed and decisions made that affected the rest of people's lives.

Like Taylor's. Did Chief Garris suspect her of being Eban's accomplice? Her fingerprints had been found in his car. She had been out running when Avis was hit, an activity with no witnesses.

The door at the end of the long, narrow hall rattled open, and Garris appeared. "Miss Taylor Milner? Right this way."

Taylor and Brooke rose at the same time.

But the chief said, "Just Taylor, please."

With a fearful, lingering glance at her companions, Taylor shuffled down the hallway to where the chief waited. The door closed firmly behind them.

Brooke reached across the vacant chair and took Faith's hand. "Now I'm scared," she whispered.

Faith clasped Brooke's hand tightly. "Try not to worry. It will be okay."

"I hope so." Brooke took out her phone. "I'm going to research recipes so I don't have a meltdown."

An hour later, Faith got up to stretch and wandered over to read the bulletin board.

When the door rattled again, they both turned to it like prisoners sensing a reprieve.

"Good night, Miss Milner," the chief said, allowing Taylor to pass through the doorway. "We'll be in touch." He nodded to Faith and Brooke before closing the door again.

Brooke sprang to her feet. "How did it go?"

Taylor glanced at Daphne. "Let's talk outside." She charged toward the front door.

Faith and Brooke exchanged looks, then hurried after her.

On the sidewalk, Taylor paused, the warm evening breeze tossing her hair. "It was so horrible in there." Tears pooled in her eyes. "The chief didn't come right out and say it, but he suspects me of helping Eban kill Avis."

Brooke engulfed her cousin in a hug. "That's ridiculous. We know you didn't do that." After a big squeeze, she slung an arm around Taylor's shoulders. "Let's go back to Faith's and talk about it."

Faith was bursting with questions, but she kept them to herself while leading the way to her SUV. They drove in tense silence, by mutual agreement waiting to begin the discussion.

In the back seat, Taylor continued to cry. As they passed the manor, she said, "I just got a text." For a minute, she couldn't talk. Then she choked out, "They arrested Eban tonight. Murder one."

18

On autopilot, Faith navigated the vehicle the rest of the way to the cottage. What she feared had come to pass, and the shock was so deep, she felt numb.

"Murder one? That's when they think it was premeditated, right? It must have been the golf ball gun. That isn't something you see every day." Brooke was babbling, running her hands through her short hair and making it stand on end.

Faith killed the engine and sat for a moment. The situation barreled toward them with the speed and weight of a freight train. "If Eban didn't do it, then who did?"

"I can't imagine." Taylor sounded helpless. "I hate to think it's one of my other friends."

"Well, I doubt it was a stranger," Brooke said. She opened her door. "We'd better kick our investigation into high gear."

"Investigation?" Taylor opened her own door and scrambled out. "But what about the police?"

"I respect the police." Faith removed the keys and climbed out. "But once in a while they seem to need a little help. And that time is now."

"What are you thinking?" Taylor asked.

Faith had recalled something she'd heard the day Avis died. "The first thing I want to do is talk to Wolfe."

The three women crossed the gardens to Castleton Manor, the soft glow of lamps lighting their way. Moths darted and danced around the globes of light, and crickets chirped in the grass. Faith normally would have lingered to enjoy the stroll, but tonight fierce determination made her single-minded. If they couldn't clear Eban, then no doubt arrest was in the near future for Taylor. According to the witness, a woman had been driving the car, and by no stretch of the imagination had that been the masculine Eban.

They took the elevator to the third floor. By the grim look on Brooke's face, Faith guessed she felt the same steely resolve to do anything to fix this mess. Taylor stood with her head down, for once not banging away on her ever-present phone.

At the apartment, Taylor unlocked the door, having moved back to her old room the day before. "Come on in," she said. "I heard Wolfe say he was going to be working in his office tonight."

The vast living room was empty, lit only by a couple of lamps. As Faith and the others trudged across the carpet to Wolfe's office, a door to a room on their right squeaked open a crack.

"Wasn't that Avis's room?" Brooke asked. "I thought it was sealed and locked by the police."

"Looks like it's been released," Taylor said.

In mutual accord, they paused in the middle of the carpet to watch whoever it was come out of the room.

When a male figure clutching a manila envelope emerged, it was difficult to say who gasped more loudly, the women or Luis.

He dropped the envelope onto the carpet and knelt to retrieve it. "You startled me," he said with a laugh.

"And you scared us, mister," Taylor said with a giggle. She pranced across the carpet to join him, flipping her hair back.

"Hold it," Faith said. Her voice was louder and more brusque than she'd intended, but she plowed ahead. "What were you doing in Avis's room? Isn't it off-limits?"

His dark eyes were wide and guileless. "Not anymore. According to Charlotte, the police released it." Luis brandished the envelope. "I went in to get something that belongs to me."

"What is it?" Taylor asked. "Can I see?"

Luis nodded and handed her the envelope.

Taylor opened it and slid a sheaf of paper out. She fumbled, and several pages fanned to the floor. "Oops." She bent to retrieve them.

A page landed near Faith, and she picked it up. It was covered with handwritten words in red ink, and she couldn't help but notice some of them. *This is badly written drivel, overdramatic . . .*

Taylor scanned one of the pages, then looked at Luis. "Who wrote this book?"

"My mother. It's a memoir about growing up in Central America, escaping death as a refugee, and becoming an American citizen." Luis sighed. "Avis talked me into letting her see it, prattling on about how she could maybe make things up to my mother. But she was brutal in her rejection."

"I can see that," Faith said, handing him the page. "Wow, she was cruel."

The writer's lips twisted. "The worst part is, she e-mailed my mom and told her that she hated it. Shot her right down. Talk about adding insult to injury."

"She was a real jerk." Taylor skimmed another page, rapt. "Will you let me read it?"

Faith's eyes met Brooke's. "Let's go find Wolfe," Faith said.

Taylor and Luis were so engrossed in conversation that they didn't appear to notice Faith and Brooke's departure.

Once out of earshot, Faith whispered, "I think we've just found motive for Luis. Did you hear what he said? 'Shot her down'? Did he repay Avis in kind?"

"I don't like it either." Brooke turned to look at her cousin. "But I hate the idea of bursting her bubble. She really loves him."

"That's better than Taylor being accused of murder along with Eban," Faith pointed out. "I'd rather break off an engagement than go to jail." *Unless the pair had been working together all along.* Faith bit her lip, holding back this bit of speculation. No sense in hurting Brooke.

Brooke put a hand to her head and moaned. "I'm so confused. It's a mess no matter which way you turn."

"Maybe Wolfe can help us." Right now, Faith fervently hoped he'd take the entire burden off their shoulders.

They arrived at his office door, and Faith knocked.

"Come in." When they entered, Wolfe glanced up from his laptop with a look of surprise. "Faith. Brooke. I was expecting my mother." He smiled. "She went to make us a batch of lemonade."

That didn't give them much time. "Can we talk to you for a minute?" Faith asked. She glanced over at Brooke, who was chewing her bottom lip anxiously. "We wouldn't bother you at this hour, but it's really important."

"Have a seat." Wolfe circled around his desk and cleared some binders and folders off the sofa. He stacked them on a side table. "As you can see, I'm up to my ears in paperwork."

Faith perched on the sofa, Brooke beside her.

"Eban Matthews was arrested tonight," Faith stated. There wasn't time for a buildup. "For first-degree murder."

Wolfe sat in his office chair with a thump. "That's a shock. What happened?"

Mindful of Charlotte's imminent return, Faith quickly filled him in on the latest developments, with Brooke interjecting anything she left out.

"But you two think he could be innocent." Wolfe leaned back in his chair and gazed at the ceiling. "Let's say he is. So who *is* guilty?"

"Luis, maybe," Faith said. "He found the golf ball gun. Who's to say he didn't put it there? And he was practicing his driving near the clubhouse when Avis was hit."

"We just caught him coming out of Avis's room," Brooke added.

"What?" Wolfe's chair squeaked forward. "What was he doing in there?"

"His mother wrote a book that Avis was reviewing. She trashed the poor woman." Faith wrinkled her nose in disgust. "On top of that, Avis drove her out of her job at Bradley years ago."

"I see where you're going with this." Wolfe tapped a pen on the desk. "When a parent is mistreated it can arouse powerful emotions. But powerful enough to kill?"

A rap sounded on the door.

Faith's heart sank. Interrupted already?

But it wasn't Charlotte who answered the summons to enter. Instead, Oren opened the door. "Sorry, Wolfe. I didn't know you had company."

"That's all right." Wolfe waved a hand. "Join us."

Oren hovered just inside the doorway. "I won't stay long. I wanted to see if we're still on for golf tomorrow morning."

Wolfe consulted his computer calendar and nodded. "Nine o'clock."

"Great. I'll see you then." He turned to go.

"Hold on," Wolfe said. "Did you hear the news?" His face fell into somber lines. "One of our employees was arrested for Avis's murder. Eban Matthews."

Oren propped himself against the doorjamb with one hand. "Eban? I . . . I can't believe it. He's such a good young man." He tipped his head, considering. "Well, I thought he was, anyway. My, that's a shocker."

Wolfe laced his hands behind his head and rocked the chair back and forth. "Didn't he caddy for you that day? I remember hearing something about that."

The writer's gaze wandered around the room, over the paintings, the bookshelves, the evening view out the window. "He did. After we finished, I went to the pro shop." He smiled sheepishly, finally making eye contact with the others. "I wanted to reward myself with a new driver for reaching my word count this week."

That was what Faith had remembered earlier—that Oren told Chief Garris he had been looking at clubs when Avis was hit by the golf ball.

"I was at the pro shop as well," Wolfe said. "I'm surprised we didn't cross paths in there."

"Me too." Oren's gaze went back to the window. He slapped the doorjamb with both hands. "Well, I'll let you be. See you tomorrow, Wolfe."

19

"Local man arrested for murder," a radio announcer intoned.

Faith gripped the steering wheel, listening intently to the story. She was on her way to the Candle House Library, Watson riding in the front passenger seat, his preferred spot. She and Midge were meeting at the library to visit with Eileen during her lunch hour.

The story concluded with no mention of Taylor, although Chief Garris said, "Further investigation is still under way."

"Yes, it is," Faith told Watson, glancing at him. "It's not over yet." The knot in her belly belied her brave words. They had so little except speculations and suspicions.

Hildegarde. Why hadn't Faith questioned the editor's widow? She must know something, or else why had she been targeted at the racetrack?

"Good idea," she muttered to herself, making a mental note to track down the woman later.

Midge's vehicle was already in the library parking lot, and Faith pulled in beside it. Since no one was around, Faith decided to let Watson follow her on foot rather than carry him. When the parking lot was busy, having him loose made her too nervous.

She picked up the bowl of pasta salad that was her contribution to the lunch, then let Watson out.

The library was cool and quiet, the familiar and well-loved aroma of paper, ink, and wood greeting Faith like a long-lost friend. She felt a pang of longing for her own library at Castleton Manor. She hadn't realized how much she was looking forward to things getting back to normal.

"We're in here." Eileen's voice floated toward them from the back of the building.

Faith and Watson wound their way past the bookshelves to the cheerful room where employees took their breaks.

Eileen poked around in the fridge while Midge sat at the scrubbed pine table, Atticus on her lap. Next to the table, a cage held Fitz, the ferret.

Watson gave a loud meow and rushed to the cage.

Fitz chittered in response.

Everyone laughed.

"It looks like they remember each other," Eileen said. She carried several bottles of sparkling water to the table.

"I'm not surprised," Midge said. "They are both very intelligent."

"I'm glad I brought him along to see Fitz," Faith said, setting her bowl on the table next to a platter of meat and cheese and a garden salad. "How are you two? It feels like ages since I've seen you."

Midge frowned. "Okay, I guess. I'm worried about Kate. You heard what happened, right?"

"I did." Faith pulled out a chair and sat. "She confided in me and Brooke about getting fired." She didn't mention that she had been Kate's first stop.

Eileen pushed the meat platter toward Faith. "Help yourself. The country club isn't pursuing the matter, are they?"

"Not so far." Midge used tongs to transfer salad onto her plate. "But Kate is hurt and upset. Justifiably so."

Faith stabbed a slice of roast beef. "I wish I could figure out how to clear her name." She dropped it on her plate and added a slice of Swiss cheese.

"Me too," Midge said. "My little girl was brought up to be impeccably honest."

"A lot of things have gone missing over there lately. Has anyone made a list?" Eileen scooped up some of Faith's pasta salad, then handed the bowl to Midge.

"I don't know," Midge said, studying the pasta dish. She smiled at Faith. "The diced red, yellow, and orange peppers are a nice touch."

"Thanks. I try." Faith served herself a pile of leafy greens, tomatoes, and cucumbers, all from Midge's garden. "I was at the club when Oren's watch was taken. But that day was a total zoo with all the fans there. One of them might have snagged it as a souvenir."

Her aunt shook her head. "People do the strangest things." She pointed her fork at Midge. "But I have an idea. Have Kate jot down the items that disappeared with the date and then think about who was around each time. Staff and guests both. Maybe a pattern will emerge."

"Guests sign in every day," Midge said. "Maybe I can convince Marvin to let me see the guest book for the days when things were lost or stolen."

"I hope he'll cooperate," Eileen said. "It's in his best interest to figure out what's going on."

They ate quietly for a few minutes.

"This is so nice," Faith said. "I'm glad you suggested it, Eileen."

"Me too. You've been so busy I almost forgot what you look like," Eileen teased. "Charlotte Jaxon created a jam-packed schedule for this retreat, didn't she?"

"She certainly did," Faith said. "And on top of that to have Avis's murder and the attempt on Hildegarde—"

The other ladies shrieked in surprise.

"What? Do tell," Midge said, her voice sliding into a Southern cadence from her childhood.

As they continued to eat, Faith took them through recent events, detailing the incident at the racetrack, the tragedy at the country club, and Taylor and Eban's ordeal.

"You've been dealing with a mess of trouble, haven't you?" Midge patted Faith on the arm.

"I'll say." Eileen speared a lettuce leaf, chewed, and swallowed. "But this is all reminding me of a story I read."

"You're not experiencing déjà vu, are you?" Midge gave a hoot of laughter.

Eileen pierced a cherry tomato and swirled it in dressing. "No,

I'm thinking about books I've read. Remember a hit-and-run accident occurred in *The Great Gatsby* and in Luis's book too. And you're having Gatsby Week at the manor."

"I don't recall anyone getting shot in Luis's book," Faith said. "Although the characters were held up at an ATM."

"But Jay Gatsby was shot," Eileen pointed out. "By the husband of the woman hit by a car."

"Following that logic, someone else should have been shot," Midge said. "But I have no idea who. Avis wasn't married."

"Perhaps the killer is staging these events as a homage to the original works." Eileen laughed. "It sounds absurd even as I say it." She popped the tomato she'd been playing with into her mouth. "Let me dig around a bit and see if my theory holds water, okay?"

"At this point, I'll take any theory at all," Faith said. "Otherwise the wrong people might go to jail."

After exhausting the discussion of the mystery around Avis's death, the conversation moved on to lighter topics during a dessert of strawberries and whipped cream.

Feeling content in both body and mind, Faith left the library with Watson trotting beside her. She decided to take a drive through town on the way home.

Faith remembered that Eban lived near the grocery store. She crawled along the narrow streets, bumper to bumper in summer traffic. Spotting the entrance to the parking lot, she turned in and parked along the row of trees in back, where Eban said he left his car.

Faith rolled down her window. Through the line of cedar trees, she could see a row of houses and an apartment building along the adjacent street. Here and there paths between the trees revealed where foot traffic had cut through over time.

She swung around in her seat and gazed at the grocery store. It was flanked by a florist and a drugstore. In the parking lot, vehicles pulled in and out, and people pushed carts.

Faith rolled up her window and headed home. She planned to take a walk down to Castleton's little beach that afternoon and read in the sunshine. A much-needed break before the ball.

With light streaming from every window, Castleton Manor floated above the lush gardens like an ocean liner at anchor. Faith minced along the garden path, taking careful steps in golden slippers. Charlotte had insisted that she borrow the gossamer green frock she'd worn in the fashion show, and it swished around her legs, making her feel glamorous and elegant.

Even from the garden, she could hear the strains of jazz through the open French doors. The Gatsby Ball was beginning.

She also heard a rustling in the bushes, a familiar sound. She stopped, pivoted, and rested her knuckles on her hips. "Rumpy, you can't come with me tonight."

The rustling ceased, but the cat didn't appear.

Faith waited another moment, then gave up and set off again. Perhaps it had been a squirrel or a rabbit.

At the manor, she entered through the Main Hall, which was decorated to the nines with standing bouquets of flowers, strings of lights, and candelabras waiting to be lit. Faith paused to admire the stunning display. After dinner, dancing couples would fill the room, swooping and swirling by candlelight.

Guests made their way toward the banquet hall for dinner, and Faith fell into company with them. All were dressed in vintage style, the women especially glittering in beaded dresses and adorned with bangles, necklaces, and jeweled headbands. In the ambience of the historic manor, Faith could easily believe that she had stepped back in time.

At the entrance of the banquet hall, a server was checking a list for table assignments. Faith was directed to the head table, and to her delight, she was seated next to Wolfe, who hadn't arrived yet.

"Faith, you look lovely." Charlotte was resplendent in a shimmering gold gown. Diamonds that looked to be family heirlooms sparkled at her throat and ears. Beside her, Lorraine and Hildegarde were equally gorgeous in lavender and navy blue.

"Thank you. So do you." Faith reached for her chair.

"Let me do that for you." Wolfe, magnificent in white tie and tails, pulled out Faith's chair for her. He smiled at the women. "What an honor to be in such beautiful company."

Did Faith imagine it, or did his gaze linger especially on her? No matter. Her reaction was a blush that began in her chest and spread into her cheeks. "Everything is spectacular," she said to Charlotte.

"Thank you. It's been a real joy to put on this event." Charlotte glanced at the staff entrance. "I just got the high sign. Dinner is about to start."

Brooke and the executive chef stood by the doors, which opened to reveal waiters filing in with covered dishes on carts. As they quietly served the diners, Charlotte tapped on her glass with a knife and stood. She welcomed everyone to the event and asked for a moment of silence in Avis's memory.

Then the bustle of dinner began, with chatting and the clatter of silverware.

A server set a plate in front of Faith and pulled off the lid. The silver-banded white plate contained sliced roast duck, mashed potatoes topped with caramelized onions, and a warm beet salad.

Faith thanked the server, then picked up her fork. "This looks amazing."

Wolfe flicked out his napkin and placed it on his lap. "It certainly does."

"The staff has outdone themselves," Charlotte crowed. "I am so pleased."

The conversation at the table remained lighthearted during the meal, for which Faith was grateful. She wanted to savor Brooke's brainchild and remain unperturbed for a while by thoughts of finding Avis's killer. Yet as she talked and laughed with Wolfe and the others, a sense of urgency thrummed underneath the festivity. *Time is running out.*

At the end of the meal, Charlotte announced that dessert would be served on the terrace, with refreshments available during the ball.

The guests got up from their seats, moving around and chatting in groups, then drifted out of the banquet hall.

"Please excuse me," Wolfe said to Faith. "I need to speak to the musicians. May I have the first number?" His smile was deeply warm and engaging, his eyes twinkling.

Warmth blazed in her cheeks, and Faith hoped he would think it was makeup reddening her skin. "Let me consult my dance card," she managed to say.

"You do that. And leave most of the places open for me." He smiled again and walked away.

"How was dinner?" Brooke stood beside Faith's chair. She had changed out of her staff outfit and was wearing a pink chiffon dress studded with silver bugle beads.

"It was excellent." Faith smiled as she took in Brooke's attire. "You look beautiful. I'm so glad you're coming to the ball."

"Me too." Brooke performed a dance step that made the beads on her dress sway. "This dress is made for boogying."

"I'll say." Faith laughed. "So is hers."

Ivy Maxwell sashayed their way, the fringe on her peach silk dress echoing each movement. She headed straight for her grandmother, who was standing nearby talking to Lorraine and Oren.

"Hi, Nana," Ivy said. "You got your key? I need to go up to your room."

Hildegarde gave her granddaughter a hard look. "What do you need up there?" Despite her question, she foraged through her clutch and handed Ivy a key.

"I just want to chill for a while before the dance," Ivy said. "You know, make a couple of calls."

Faith considered that Ivy worked at the country club and had the run of Castleton Manor.

"Let's go talk to Ivy," Faith whispered to Brooke. "She's one person we haven't questioned."

"True. We'll give her time to get upstairs, and then we'll follow."

They lingered for a couple of minutes before hurrying after Ivy. The indicator on the elevator showed Ivy had made it to the top floor.

"Let's not wait for it to come down," Brooke said. She took the stairs two at a time, even in her heels.

Faith did her best to keep up.

On the third floor, the entrance to the apartment stood open. Charlotte had invited Faith to feel at home, so she felt only slightly squeamish going inside.

"This place is huge," Brooke said. "Where's Hildegarde's room?"

"As far as I know the guests are in the front suites," Faith replied. "Follow me."

They crossed the foyer, heels clattering on the marble, and entered a corridor lined with doors.

Ivy was fumbling with the key in front of one of the rooms.

"Need some help?" Brooke offered. "Some of the locks in this place are sticky."

Ivy jumped. "Where did you two come from?" She managed to insert the key and turned it with a click.

"We hoped we could talk to you for a minute," Faith said.

"About what?" Ivy twisted the knob and pushed the door open. "Come on in."

Hildegarde's room was lushly appointed with thick carpet and matching upholstery, bedding, and lacy curtains trimming the tall windows. Jewelry was scattered across the dresser top, and as Faith edged into the room, she spotted something interesting.

"Excuse me for a second." Ivy popped into the adjacent bathroom and closed the door. "I'll be right out," she called.

Faith took advantage of her absence to check the items on the dresser. A velvet cloth had been laid out to display necklaces, bracelets, and earrings. Her heart pounded when she noticed opal post earrings, with the center stone surrounded by diamonds. Surely she was wrong. After all, there were millions of similar earrings in the world.

"Do you see those earrings?" she whispered to Brooke.

"Those look like Kate's. Let's find out." Brooke opened her bag and pulled out her phone to snap a photo.

The bathroom knob rattled.

"Hurry," Faith urged. She slid closer to the door, hoping to block Ivy's view.

Ivy appeared startled to see Faith standing right by the door when she emerged. "Did you need to go in?"

"No, I'm fine," Faith said. She took a covert glance over her shoulder at Brooke, who was now texting. *Whew.* "So you've been editing Luis's book. Do you work for a publisher?"

"Why? Are you interested in becoming an editor?" Ivy looked Faith up and down. "You have to have certain skills."

Faith, irked by this condescension, crossed her arms. "I have advanced degrees in library science with a concentration in literature. I think I have skills."

"You might." Ivy brushed past Faith. "I love editing. It's like being a sculptor, only with words. And since you asked, I'm freelance editing right now. But I'm not going to be treated the way my grandfather was." She went to the bureau where Brooke still stood and nudged her aside.

Faith's heart leaped into her throat. Was Ivy onto them? But no, the younger woman started opening the drawers and searching through the stacks of clothing inside.

"What are you doing?" Brooke asked, stepping out of the way.

Ivy's smile was sly. "Nana keeps money around, and I need to borrow some." She unrolled a pair of tennis socks, revealing a roll of bills. "See?" She tucked the money into the beaded bag she wore slung around her shoulders.

Faith was offended on Hildegarde's behalf. "That's not very nice."

"Neither am I." Ivy glared at her. "But it's none of your business. Why did you follow me up here again?"

Brooke, who had been studying her phone, gave a crow of satisfaction. She waved it at the other two. "We need to go find Hildegarde."

Ivy's glare became a scowl. "Why? To tell on me?" Her tone was mocking. "Good luck with that. Nana adores me."

"It's nothing to do with you," Brooke said. "I think." She pointed to the opal earrings, glowing softly on the velvet. "Your grandmother has Kate Foster's earrings. We need to find out where she got them."

A succession of emotions raced over Ivy's face—confusion, concern, horror. "Oh no, you're not pinning the theft on me. I had nothing to do with it."

Faith, who believed that very thing, temporized. Although judging by Ivy's interest in money, she probably would have sold the earrings. "We're not accusing anyone of anything. Let's go find your grandmother and ask her. Maybe she bought them at a pawnshop." That scenario created a surreal picture in Faith's mind, but she wanted to keep the situation calm.

Ivy flounced toward the door. "Fine with me. She'll clear this up. I'm sure they're hers and your theory is just plain wrong."

They took the stairs to the second floor, pausing on the balcony to watch the activity in the Great Hall Gallery. The orchestra was playing a lively Charleston, and couples kicked and pranced around the floor, reminding Faith of cavorting children.

Faith scanned the crowd for Hildegarde, who was distinctive with her silver hair and navy blue dress. "I don't see your grandmother anywhere." Wolfe wasn't on the dance floor either. *Is he waiting for me?* She thrust that thought aside. They had more pressing issues at the moment.

"Oh well," Ivy said. "She's got to be around here somewhere. Catch you later." With that farewell, she skipped down the flight of stairs, the fringe on her dress bouncing.

"I can tell she's really concerned," Brooke said drily.

"Maybe she's hiding her true feelings," Faith said. "She was pretty surprised when you confronted her with those earrings."

Brooke started down the steps. "I saw Charlotte over near the Agatha Christie statue. Maybe she knows where her friend is."

Faith followed, then halted when her phone rang in her bag. "I'm going to check that. Go on ahead and I'll catch up." She couldn't imagine who was calling, and by the time she fumbled the phone out, it had gone to voice mail. *Eileen.* She checked the message, which simply said, "Call me."

It can probably wait. Still holding the phone, Faith continued down the steps.

A text buzzed onto the screen. Eileen again. *It's urgent. Call me now.*

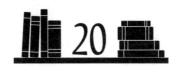

20

Faith stared at the text, blinking as she read it again. She'd better find out what Eileen wanted because her aunt was not one to overstate a situation. She hurried back up the stairs, seeking a quiet corner since the orchestra was in full swing. The open gallery's high ceilings and marble surfaces amplified the jazz tune.

At the end of the corridor she chose a chair placed next to a potted palm and dialed her aunt.

"Faith, I'm so glad you called." Eileen sounded breathless with excitement. "You won't believe what I pieced together."

"I'm all ears," Faith said.

"What's that in the background?" Eileen asked as the brass section gave an extra loud *blat*.

"The orchestra." Faith got up from the chair and wandered deeper into the building to find a quieter spot. A room where linens were stored was open, so she walked in. As she closed the door, a flash of color went past. A guest? They probably thought she was really strange going into the closet. "Go ahead."

"After our lunch I got to thinking about how there had to be a connection between the hit-and-run accident and the golf ball."

"That was the most confusing aspect of the whole thing. I thought there might be two people working independently." Faith gave a humorless laugh. "Imagine being so disliked that two people try to kill you." She paced back and forth, one corner of her mind admiring the snowy towers of folded towels and sheets on the shelves.

"And I thought maybe the golf ball *was* an accident, fortuitous for the killer. Until they found that gun." Eileen sighed. "I went around and around, same as you. Eventually I decided to simply start with what we know—that the incidents resembled the plots of books written by authors at the event. Or by F. Scott Fitzgerald. Are you with me so far?"

"I am. Keep going." Excitement and impatience were building, but she kept them in check. Eileen was a methodical person, and she liked to explain the trail she had followed.

"We found hit-and-run accidents in Luis's book and *The Great Gatsby*. But guess what?" Eileen paused. "One of Oren's books features death by golf ball. A disillusioned executive meets his demise on the course."

"What? Why didn't he say something when Avis died?"

Eileen echoed her thought. "It's very odd, right? Of course it would be quite audacious—if not stupid—to choose a cause of death you'd written about in one of your famous books."

"True. So you don't think he did it?"

Eileen sighed. "No. I did a little more digging about some of the other people staying at Castleton. A librarian friend of mine in New York helped. She has access to industry periodicals that most libraries don't carry."

"Industry? You mean publishing?"

"That's right. I discovered that Francis Maxwell was abruptly forced out of his job just before retirement."

Francis Maxwell. Hildegarde's husband. "Wow. I didn't know."

"Yes, Avis went over his head and complained to the publisher when Francis had a conflict with one of her authors. Since she brought them many of their best-selling writers, she had quite a lot of influence. It got ugly, with Francis threatening to file a lawsuit for wrongful termination. Soon after he left, he had a heart attack and died."

Sympathy stabbed Faith, despite the direction the story was leading. "Poor Hildegarde." Her whole life had fallen apart, and within a short time she'd gone from being the wife of a respected man to an impoverished exile.

"It's very sad. Soon afterward, their New York apartment was repossessed, and Hildegarde left the city for a small town in Connecticut."

Faith gasped. "That's why she's been stealing. Either out of need or envy. We found Kate's earrings in her room tonight."

"Really? That's very interesting, but I think we have a bigger problem on our hands. I believe Hildegarde killed Avis." Eileen's tone sharpened. "And that's not all. An article that came out two days ago claims Oren and Lorraine Edwards were instrumental in having Francis fired. Avis's death led a tabloid reporter to dig into her career, and that dreadful incident was rehashed. The couple might be in danger."

Faith's heart gave a huge, painful jolt. *Is the killer floating around the ball in a blue dress?* "You really think Hildegarde is guilty."

"I don't have proof, but it all fits. My gut is telling me I'm right."

More pieces clicked in Faith's mind. *The drugstore Hildegarde went to the morning of the hit-and-run accident is near Eban's house. She must have stolen Eban's car and hit Avis. Then she abandoned it and returned to her own, shopped, and drove back to the manor. How clever.* "Mine too. What do you think she'll do?"

Eileen's voice was grim. "I have no idea, but I still have one of Oren's books to scan. I'll call if I figure something out."

"Please do. I'll go warn them." Faith turned the doorknob and pushed, but the door didn't budge. "Hang on. There's something wrong with the door." She set the phone down on a shelf and put her shoulder into it. The door remained immobile. Had she accidentally locked it? She snatched up the phone. "Eileen, I'm stuck in a linen closet."

"Closet?" Eileen squawked. "What are you doing in a closet?"

"I came in here to talk because it's quiet. I'd better go. If you don't hear back from me in ten minutes, send someone to rescue me." Faith disconnected and texted Brooke. *Help. Second-floor linen closet. East corridor.* She had to get out of here fast. She called the front desk.

First the phone rang forever. When the clerk finally answered, he thought she was playing a prank and hung up.

She tried calling Brooke, but it went straight to voice mail. She'd never hear the phone above the music. *Surely she must be wondering where I am.*

Out of desperation, Faith texted Wolfe. *Meet me at the second-floor linen closet in the east corridor. I need help.*

Now that was cryptic. She hoped he would see it and respond.

Out of instinct more than anything, Faith pounded on the door. Fruitless. No one was around, and the door was thick and well-made, like everything at Castleton.

What if Wolfe or Brooke comes and I don't hear them? She couldn't bang on the door much longer. Her fists already hurt. She paced around and around the small space, grateful that at least there was a light. She looked at the pillowcases, then the crack under the door. A shelf held other tools of the housekeeping trade, including an inventory list and a pen. *A pen.*

Yes! Grabbing the writing implement, Faith did a little victory dance. There was no room to scribble on the list, so, with a wince and a silent apology to Marlene, she defaced a gorgeous sheet with ink.

I'm stuck in this closet. Help.

Faith

Kneeling carefully in her gown, she slid the cloth under the door so the letters would be visible from the other side. A few more circuits of the closet and she was rewarded by the murmur of voices on the other side of the door. Heedless of her bruises, she banged on the wood, shouting.

Another few seconds and the door opened, revealing the amazed faces of Wolfe and Brooke. A heavy table had been pushed into the middle of the hall. That must have been what had blocked the door.

Faith didn't even allow herself to sag in relief. She burst out of the closet and said, "Don't just stand there. We have a killer to catch."

As the trio raced along the corridor, Faith filled them in on her conversation with Eileen. Both were quick studies and understood her gasped explanations.

"Hildegarde killed Avis and may now be after Lorraine and Oren," Wolfe stated. "Got it."

They were almost to the bottom of the grand staircase when they spotted Lorraine trudging up.

Faith clattered down to her. "Are you all right?"

The older woman eyed her strangely. "Yes, I'm a little tired, but the ball is wonderful." She turned to Brooke. "And dinner was scrumptious."

"Where's your husband?" Wolfe asked. "Is he on his way?"

She drew back, obviously confused.

He added, "I was hoping to engage him in a game of billiards."

Lorraine waved a hand, laughing. "Good luck with that. He'll cream you."

"So where is he? Do you know?" Wolfe persisted.

The writer's wife peered down into the milling crowd, a frown creasing her brow. "You know, I haven't actually seen him for a while. I'm not sure."

"Lorraine." Wolfe's tone was low but urgent. "We need to find your husband right away." He swallowed. "He may be in danger."

"In danger? What on earth are you talking about?" Lorraine glanced around, as though seeking answers. Her face filled with anguish as awareness dawned. "Do you mean someone might try to kill him, like they did Avis? I knew our sins would come back to haunt us."

Faith exchanged glances with Brooke. Eileen was right.

"Sins or not, we must find Oren and Hildegarde." Wolfe gestured for them to come closer. "We must be discreet. No sense in creating a panic."

"When did you last see your husband?" Faith asked. "Or Hildegarde?"

Lorraine wrung her hands. "Not since dinner. Oren said he had some calls to make. I haven't seen Hildegarde since we left the banquet hall."

"Go up and check your room," Wolfe said. "Then call me."

"And you call me if you find him." Lorraine started climbing again, moving at a much more rapid pace.

"Now what?" Faith asked Wolfe. She studied the crowd. It would be impossible to find anyone in that crush.

"I've thought of a shortcut." Wolfe's smile was smug. "I'm going to give out tickets to a ride in my private plane. To Oren and Hildegarde. If they're still at the ball, they'll come forward."

"Great idea," Brooke said. "Faith and I will circle the room and ask if anyone has seen them."

Wolfe nodded. "If they're not in here, meet me by the stage. We'll go on to plan B. Before you ask, I'm trying to figure out what that is right now."

Faith and Brooke split up at the foot of the stairs. Moving fast but trying to appear casual, Faith scanned the people on the fringes of the dance floor and those on it but didn't spot Oren or Hildegarde.

She pushed her way to the Agatha Christie statue. Charlotte was still holding forth with a group of friends.

When Faith arrived at the edge of the circle, Charlotte greeted her effusively. "Are you having an absolutely fabulous time? You must be." She radiated delight and satisfaction. "This event is all I dreamed it could be."

Faith injected enthusiasm into her voice. "It's wonderful. But may I speak to you a minute? There's a . . . slight issue." *Of murder.*

"Of course. I'll be right back, ladies."

When Wolfe's mother joined her a few paces away, Faith asked, "Have you seen Oren or Hildegarde?" She attempted to keep her voice light and casual, but despite her efforts, a quaver crept in.

Charlotte's blissful expression vanished. "What is it? Something's happened. I can tell by your face."

"Not yet. We think. We're hoping to—"

Feedback from a microphone interrupted. "Sorry about that," Wolfe said. "First day with a new microphone."

The crowd laughed.

"For those of you who don't know, I'm Wolfe Jaxon, co-owner of this lovely place with my mother, Charlotte."

Clapping and whistles of appreciation echoed in the chamber.

How can he act so calm? Anyone listening would never guess that he was on the trail of a killer.

"I hope you're all having fun," Wolfe went on, "but I have some contest winners to announce. Oh, you didn't know there was a contest? Well, we entered all your names in a drawing, and the winners will receive a private plane tour of the coast, complete with meal service."

Charlotte sidled closer to Faith. "What's this about? I don't recall him ever mentioning a contest. And is he talking about giving people a ride in his plane? How strange."

Wolfe continued. "And the lucky winners are . . . drumroll, please. Hildegarde Maxwell and Oren Edwards. Please come forward."

Nothing happened. The lights swept over the crowd, but Oren and Hildegarde were nowhere to be found.

"I guess we'll have to catch up with them later," Wolfe said. "Have a good evening, folks." He relinquished the microphone back to the bandleader.

"That's my cue," Faith said to Charlotte, who looked puzzled. "We'll explain later." With a wave and a smile, she plunged into the throng.

On the other side of the room, Faith glimpsed Brooke also working her way to Wolfe. He stood by the stage searching for them.

Her phone vibrated in her bag. Something told her to check. Eileen again. But it was too loud in the room to call her so Faith decided to wait.

"That was a bust," Wolfe said when she and Brooke joined him. "And Lorraine said neither of them is upstairs. I'm not getting a good feeling about this."

Brooke shook her head. "Where do we begin? This place is enormous, both indoors and out."

Faith pulled out her phone. "Eileen called. Let's step out on the terrace and see what she has to say."

"Might as well." Wolfe headed in that direction. "We don't have anything else."

Out on the terrace, Faith called Eileen and put her on speakerphone so the others could hear. "Oren and Hildegarde have disappeared," Faith blurted out.

Eileen sucked in a breath. "Uh-oh. Get down to the beach quick. The last book Francis edited for Oren featured a man who killed himself—by filling his pockets with rocks and jumping into the water."

21

"We're on it, Eileen," Faith said. She clicked off. "Let's go."

"Hang on," Wolfe said, retrieving his own phone from his tuxedo jacket. "Let me call Chief Garris." He placed the brief call, then tucked the phone away.

Faith, Brooke, and Wolfe tramped down the terrace steps and entered the garden. Wolfe led the way, guiding them through a maze of paths to the cliff top, where a flight of stairs went down to the water. At times Faith heard rustling in the bushes, but when she turned to look she saw nothing. She hoped Watson was keeping out of trouble.

"I haven't been at this end too often," Faith said, keeping her voice low. Voices carried along the beach despite the ocean breeze and constant murmur of waves rolling onto the shore.

"It's not a very nice beach," Wolfe said. "Rocky, with lots of seaweed. Most people prefer the sandy one." He took the first step. "Careful now. Use the railing." Within seconds, he descended into darkness, only the pale, luminescent ocean and sandy cliff providing some contrast.

Faith's heels proved tricky, so she stopped and slipped them off. "Take off your shoes," she said to Brooke, who was behind her. "It's easier to walk." Holding the shoes in one hand and the railing in the other, Faith stepped down onto warm, silky boards, one after the other. After what seemed like hours, she reached the pebbled shore.

A dark shape detached itself from the rock face. Wolfe. "Quiet now," he whispered. "They're over there." He pointed to the edge of the water. "It looks like we barely made it in time."

A light beamed on, revealing Oren standing in water up to his thighs, incoming swells rising even higher. Perched on a huge, flat boulder, Hildegarde trained the flashlight and—to Faith's horror—a gun on the writer.

"Go on. Pick up more rocks," Hildegarde growled hoarsely, waving the gun at Oren. "You should know how it's done since you wrote about it." She cackled.

Oren bent and picked up one tiny rock and added it to his sagging pockets. "Why are you doing this? I'm sorry. We never intended to hurt Francis—"

"Shut up! You got my husband fired from the job that was his life. Why wouldn't that hurt him?" Hildegarde's voice rose in pitch to almost a shriek. "And then he *died*!"

"I'm sorry," Oren repeated, raising his hands in surrender. "I'll do whatever I can to make it up to you."

"Your death will make it up to me." The cackle rang out again. "And guess what? You gave me an idea for a book. Your little mystery about a dead agent inspired my first chapter, and your novel about a suicidal writer will provide the climax."

Oren whimpered, his shoulders shaking.

Wolfe's voice thundered out. "Drop the gun, Hildegarde, and let him go. It's over."

Hildegarde whipped her head around. "How perfect. The rescue party arrives. But you can't do a thing. Move closer and I'll shoot him."

"Help is on the way," Wolfe said. "The police will be here any minute. Stop before you commit another murder."

Hildegarde waved the gun. "Or two or three." She laughed. "As you noticed the other day, I'm a very good shot. Francis and I used to go on safari. Although I regret shooting elephants, it was good practice for Avis, and I have no regrets about that."

"She's crazy," Brooke whispered to Faith.

"No kidding." Faith prayed Hildegarde wouldn't decide to shoot at them.

"I'm serious," Wolfe said. "I called the police."

"So I'll give them some work. If they can find the body. It might drift out to sea." Hildegarde lifted the gun.

Faith held her breath as she waited for the inevitable report. But she heard only rocks tumbling and bouncing down the cliff, some landing in the water with a splash.

Hildegarde flinched and looked in the direction of the noise.

Wolfe took advantage of her distraction and launched himself at her. The gun went flying, landing with a clatter of metal, and he and Hildegarde fell into the surf.

Faith darted forward and grabbed the gun. "Oren, get out of the water!" she yelled to the writer, who stood frozen in place, watching as Wolfe and Hildegarde struggled.

"Forget that!" With a roar, Oren joined the fray, helping Wolfe subdue Hildegarde.

Together they wrestled her to the beach. Wolfe pulled off his tie and bound her hands. Oren used his to secure her ankles.

"That should do it." Wolfe brushed the sand off his hands. "I'd better tell the police where we are." He reached for his phone, then patted his pocket in chagrin. "Oops. I must have lost it in the water."

"Use mine," Faith said. She dug it out of her bag.

"You'll never get away with this!" Hildegarde screeched. "I know a good attorney."

"You'll need one," Wolfe said drily. He stepped away a few feet to place the call.

Oren crouched beside Hildegarde, water dripping from his ruined tuxedo. "I'm sorry, Hildy. It's no excuse, but you know that once Avis got on a roll there was no stopping her. I was weak to go along with it. Please forgive me."

Hildegarde sneered at him. "Bah. Save it for one of your books. By the way, they were lousy without my Francis editing your work. That's why your sales have plummeted since he died."

The writer's eyes went wide, the arrow of self-doubt having found its mark. He rose and stumbled away toward the stairs.

"You sabotaged your own race car, didn't you?" Faith asked Hildegarde. Now that the woman was safely restrained, she wanted to clear up a few things.

Hildegarde laughed. "Of course. I'm far too good a driver to miss something so obvious as a loose wheel."

"Or to accidentally hit someone." Faith's stomach churned. "You stole Eban's car from the parking lot." She had guessed that but wanted to hear it from Hildegarde.

I was going to hot-wire the car, but the idiot left a key under the mat." Hildegarde's brow creased. "I did misplace that key somewhere."

"We found it. Actually my cat did," Faith said. "And all those missing items at the country club."

"Yes, that was me. Careless fools deserve to lose their things, all of them."

"You wrote those nasty letters to Avis, didn't you?" Faith persisted.

Hildegarde smirked. "I was an aspiring writer myself once too, you know."

A soft meow reached her ears, and she turned to see Watson padding across the sand. He rubbed himself against Faith's ankles, purring.

Faith reached down to pat him, then glanced at the cliff. She scooped him up. "You helped us, didn't you, Rumpy? What a good boy you are."

Once again the cat had come through for his owner. A simple matter of creating an avalanche, a technique he'd learned from a Saint Bernard friend. Deft paws and a good eye—even at night—were all that was needed. The bad lady, the one he'd scratched in the bushes and followed into

the locker room, was tied up on the sand. She wouldn't be hurting anyone again. And his ferret friend was avenged at last.

The cat ratcheted up his purr to the highest level. He and his person could save the world if they had to.

Soft jazz played by the orchestra on the terrace drifted through Castleton's gardens. With Wolfe at her side, Faith sauntered down a path illuminated by glowing lanterns. The air was soft and warm, and the breeze carried the fragrance of night-blooming flowers and salt water.

"What a gorgeous night," she said. "I'm glad we came out here."

By the time the police took Hildegarde away, Faith and Wolfe had missed the ball. Despite the exhausted crash that came after heightened excitement and danger, Faith had readily agreed when Wolfe suggested a midnight stroll. To her delight, he'd asked the musicians to stay on for a while.

"Wait until you see this." Taking her arm, Wolfe steered her onto a side path, a route Faith recognized as leading to the lavender pocket garden.

A rustling in the bushes informed her that Watson had joined them. She smiled at the thought of her furry chaperone. *He wants to keep an eye on me.*

"After you." Wolfe gestured for Faith to enter the garden first.

She stepped through the opening in the hedge and gasped.

"Isn't it spectacular?" he said, moving to stand beside her.

The full moon rode just above the horizon, golden light reflecting in the dark water below. They watched in silence as the silver orb climbed the heavens.

"What an adventure we had tonight," Wolfe said. He leaned a tiny bit closer. "You make the best . . . teammate."

Why did she sense he had been about to say something else? She smiled at him. "Maybe we ought to pick a different sport."

Wolfe laughed. "I couldn't agree more."

Faith felt Watson slide past her calf. She picked him up for a cuddle, her heart filled with contentment. A mystery solved, a moonlit summer night, and two friends by her side. Nothing could be better.

Watson purred in agreement.

Up to this point, we've been doing all the writing. Now it's *your* turn!

Tell us what you think about this book, the characters, the bad guy, or anything else you'd like to share with us about this series. We can't wait to hear from *you*!

Log on to give us your feedback at:
https://www.surveymonkey.com/r/CastletonLibrary